Karen Louise Hollis was b   rought
up in a house full of noteb   r
parents being journalists.

Her first self-published boo   Un-
Conventional: 13 Years of N   who was
published by Hirst Books in   and subsequently republished by
Lulu. Her biography of the actor Anthony Ainley was published by
Fantom Publishing in 2015 and is available in hardback, paperback
and audio CD.

She lives in Lincoln with her mother, her son and her cat and enjoys
writing, reading, sewing, politics, history and watching gymnastics.
This is her first novel.

karenlouisehollis.co.uk to buy my books

BOOK BLOG: iheartbooks.blog

TWITTER: @KarenLNHollis

Also by Karen Louise Hollis

POETRY AND SHORT STORIES
Decades
From Darkness Through Light
Tales of Dark Nights, Death and Violent Encounters
Petals of Pleasure … Petals of Pain

GYMNASTICS
A Golden Era of Gymnastics 1980-84
A Golden Era of Gymnastics 1985-89
Gymnasts in Conversation – Volume One
Gymnasts in Conversation – Volume Two
Gymnasts in Conversation – Volume Three
Gymnasts in Conversation – Volume Four
USSR Gymnasts in Conversation
Romanian Gymnasts in Conversation
American Gymnasts in Conversation
Bulgarian Gymnasts in Conversation
Alexei Tikhonkikh in Conversation

MOTHERHOOD
Thoughts of a New Old Mum

BIOGRAPHY
The Man Behind the Master – Anthony Ainley

DOCTOR WHO
Un-Conventional: 13 Years of Meeting the Stars of Doctor Who
The Other Side of the Table

Welcome to Whitlock Close

by
Karen Louise Hollis

First published in Great Britain in 2022

Copyright © Karen Louise Hollis

This novel is entirely a work of fiction. The names, characters and incidents portrayed in it are the work of the author's imagination. Any resemblance to actual persons, living or dead, events or localities is entirely coincidental.

The moral right of Karen Louise Hollis to be identified as the author of this work has been asserted in accordance with the Copyright, Designs and Patents Act of 1988.

All rights reserved. No part of this publication may be reproduced, stored in a retrieval system, or transmitted in any form or by any means, electronic, mechanical, photocopying, recording, or otherwise, without the prior permission of both the copyright owner and the above publisher of this book.

Cover artwork © by Julie Forester

https://julieforesterbooks.simdif.com

ACKNOWLEDGEMENTS

Thanks to my family and friends who support me on my writing journey, especially my dad Peter Brown and my sister Elizabeth Train-Brown, who are both excellent writers.

To Anita Faulkner and her Chick Lit and Prosecco Facebook group for their general help and inspiration.

To all the authors I talk to online, especially on Twitter who inspire me in so many ways – Abigail Yardimci, Hazel Prior, Penny Batchelor, Joanna Toye, Heidi Swain, Samantha Tonge, Lewis Hastings, Amanda James, Judy Leigh, Jessica Redland, Tina Baker, Frances Quinn – oh, so many, I can't remember them all. But read all their books, they're brilliant!

To the great people on Twitter, especially the Book Community, Writing Community and my Twitter Sisters.

Thanks to Gela Louise Fossett for allowing me to use the name of her family circus (Fossett's Circus) in the book.

Thanks to Nick Headley for his computer wizardry.

To the 1980s, especially the USSR women's gymnastics team from the 1980 Olympics who changed my life in so many ways –

Elena Davydova
Natalia Shaposhnikova
Stella Zakharova
Nelli Kim
Maria Filatova
And the late great Elena Naimushina

LIST OF MAIN CHARACTERS

1 Whitlock Close – Old Mr White

3 Whitlock Close – Robert Thorpe (journalist, 36), his wife Sandra (36) and their daughter Louise (11)

5 Whitlock Close – Sarah Willington (school teacher, mid-twenties)

7 Whitlock Close – Gerry Smallacre (41) and his wife Chloe (41)

9 Whitlock Close – Dr Chidi Achebe (GP, 49), his wife Beatrice (48) and their children Faith (15), Grace (12), Raymond (10) and Noah (6)

11 Whitlock Close – Hugh (50, actor and TV presenter)

13 Whitlock Close – Nora (76), widow

15 Whitlock Close – Mabel (74), widow

July 1981

The Thorpe family were on holiday in a caravan in Ingoldmells when the police arrived. Two of them – one man and one woman. 'Mr. and Mrs. Thorpe?' they asked. Robert and Sandra nodded anxiously, everything rushing through their heads from whether their mothers had died to that time in June when Rob had been slightly over the speed limit. Neither of them expected to hear the words that came out of the policeman's mouth.

'I'm afraid your house has been hit by lightning. It's on fire.'

'Oh my God!' Robert said, as Sandra lost the strength in her legs and partially collapsed against the caravan door.

Their daughter Louise pushed between them. 'Has everything in my bedroom been destroyed?' She was mentally thinking of all her precious possessions. She had only brought a few things to the caravan with her, as they were only staying four days.

The policewoman smiled sympathetically. 'We don't know all the details yet, I'm sorry. The lightning hit the roof, the neighbours rang 999 and the fire brigade are there now, trying to stop it. Hopefully it won't be as bad as it could have been.'

The police left about ten minutes later. They had been kind and sympathetic, but only knew so much. The Thorpes were left to decide what to do next, each imagining the worst scenario.

'Let's pack!' Rob took the lead. 'We're going to want to see what's happening.'

'It's almost nine. Should I ring my mother now, before she goes to bed? We might need to stay at hers for a few days.'

'Yes, good idea. Explain the situation.'

Sandra went to the phone box at the far end of the caravan site, while Rob and Louise began packing. It was just over an hour's drive from Ingoldmells to their home in Lincoln.

Louise spoke carefully, trying to keep her composure. She was eleven years old after all, not a baby. 'I don't think I want to see our house if it's on fire, Dad.'

'That's okay, love, we'll take you straight to Grandma's.'

Sandra came back from the phone box looking a bit more relieved. 'Yes, that's all sorted, she's making up the spare beds and is happy to have us to stay as long as we need to.'

'Brilliant!' Rob gave her a hug. 'We've almost finished packing, so we can get off soon. Louise wants to stay with Gran, so you and I can have a look at the house, see what's what.'

They were starting to feel a bit better. At least they had a plan, something to do.

Then Louise let out a strange, distressed whimper. Her parents both looked at her.

'What about the cat?'

Gran was pleased to see them all and insisted Rob and Sandra have a cup of tea before setting off to see their house. After they'd left, she showed Louise into the bedroom and told her to make herself at home. She loved staying in this bedroom because it had all of her grandma's old books from when she was young. There were old school stories and books about a young nurse, hardbacks with exciting titles like *Shirley Flight - Air Hostess and The Diamond Smugglers*. But tonight, she didn't want to read. She wanted to know if her cat Mitty was okay and all her things in her bedroom – her dolls, books and the cuddly toys she'd had since birth.

Her parents arrived back about an hour later, carrying Mitty in a plastic cat carrier. They handed him to Louise. 'He's fine, he's just been wandering around the street, crying. He came straight over to us. Mrs. Cross lent us the cat carrier and he was happy to go in it for once!'

They all went through to the sitting room and sat round the table. After a quick cuddle, Mitty jumped down and went off to explore this house he had never seen before.

Rob started explaining what the situation was. 'We spoke to the fire brigade, it's all under control now and luckily, the damage was confined to the roof and the loft. They think the lightning strike caused a fireball in the loft, but it was contained there and didn't go down to the lower floors.'

'So our things are okay?' Louise was much brighter now.

'Pretty much. The loft contents are gone. Things like our Christmas tree and decorations. Some old papers and stuff. I think there was a bag of your baby clothes, bits like that.'

'But it could have been much worse!' added Sandra.

'When can you go in and get your belongings?' asked Gran.

'Not sure yet, the fire brigade will ring us. I've given them your number. They think we'll need the roof completely rebuilding, so I'm afraid we may be here a while.'

'That's perfectly fine, you know you're all welcome here as long as you need to stay. It'll be a pleasure having you.'

The cat reappeared from his travels and looked up at Gran expectantly. 'Meow!' he said.

'Yes, you too, Puss!'

Later that week, when Rob and Sandra were alone, Sandra decided it was time for a talk.

'I don't want to go back to the house.'

'What do you mean, love? You want to wait till it's all repaired?'

'No. I want to move.'

'Oh.'

'You know we weren't sure about the secondary school here? Well, if we moved to somewhere else, Louise could start at a better school.'

'Where were you thinking of? Anywhere in particular?'

'New Barnham. The school is excellent there. I think we deserve a new start.'

September 1981

Her new school looked huge! She wasn't the tallest eleven-year-old in the world anyway and as the house move had been fairly last minute, Louise Thorpe hadn't had the chance to go round the school before starting there. Her dad had dropped her off at the gate and she had shooed him away before anyone could see. All the other kids seemed to be walking in with friends, a few of the older girls hand in hand with boyfriends. But she didn't have one friend. No wonder she felt sick. Her mother had insisted she eat something before leaving the house, but she only managed a slice of white bread with nothing on it and half a cup of tea. She just hoped she wouldn't see it again on the way up!

They had moved in August 1981, after the house fire, and now lived at 3 Whitlock Close in the village of New Barnham. The Close was a quiet cul-de-sac in a fairly new bit of a pleasant estate. There were eight semi-detached houses and each one had a driveway and a front garden. It was tidy with well-kept trees and flowerbeds - the sort of area her mother had always longed to live in, as it looked quite posh and middle class. Class was important to Louise's mother.

By the start of the Autumn school term, the Thorpes had only lived in the village a couple of weeks and that had been spent getting everything exactly like it had been in their old house, but in the new one. Louise spent a lot of time complaining to herself and wishing they could just have relocated their old home here and saved a lot of bother. It was a bigger house now, but their old one was a three-storey Victorian terraced, so they had still had lots of room. She used to do two cartwheels in a row across her yellow carpeted bedroom floor, but here her furniture took up too much of the floor space. She would have to practice her gymnastics downstairs where the front room and dining room had been knocked through into one long room. If she was allowed to move the dining table back a bit, she could maybe get three tumbling skills in.

They had briefly met their immediate neighbours. Old Mr. White (as he was called by everyone, they soon learned) lived at number one, he had seemingly been there forever and was rumoured to be not far off ninety. He had outlived his wife by twenty-odd years, but still seemed relatively fit and happy.

On the other side of them, separated by their driveways, was Sarah Willington at number five. She was young, probably mid-twenties and was a primary school teacher in a nearby village. She seemed to be away long hours, so they hadn't seen much of her, but she always smiled and waved when they did and remembered their names.

Louise missed her old home, she had been there since birth and although it was in the city, she had been right near the West Common which held lots of memories for her – watching the horses grazing (so inspiring, she'd written a prize-winning poem about it at her old school!), going to the park and the ornamental pond with her dad at weekends, big Bonfire Night parties where she would try to spot her school friends in the dark while eating mushy peas from polystyrene pots. There was a big park across the Common too with swings, a big slide and other play equipment she loved climbing on.

She'd only had a little back yard at home, but she had made the most of it. There was a coal bunker at the top which seemed completely useless by the 1970s, but she used the little wall they had as a beam and her parents had bought her a swing. Being an only child meant she had to amuse herself a lot of the time, but she found that easy. She spent hours on that swing, singing and jumping off at the highest point, practicing a perfect landing. She'd have friends over and they'd do gymnastics or sing along to Abba and Blondie, inventing their own dance routines and putting on concerts for Louise's parents.

Her first and middle schools had been pretty good, she had enjoyed them overall, but when it became time to move up to secondary school, her parents weren't happy. The school she was due to go to was "full of rough kids" according to her mother. Then the fire had been the final straw; none of them really wanted to go back after that. Her mum was the boss, so Dad concurred, and they moved out of the city, seven miles away to a nice house with a big garden in a quiet cul-de-sac.

They took their black and white cat Mitty with them. (She had originally called it Mitzi as a kitten, only to later find out it was a male!) To help Louise settle into the new situation, her parents soon bought her a Cavalier King Charles Spaniel puppy. Her mother wanted to call her Lady Diana (She was a big fan!), Louise wanted to call her Olga Korbut (Yes, a gymnastics fan!), so they compromised on Lady Olga. Mitty didn't mind, it was company, and they were about the same size.

All this was going round her head as she walked through the school gates and looked around at the big blocks of similar looking buildings, having no idea where to go or what to do. She saw a group of small girls giggling together and ran up to them. 'Are you in the First Year?'

'Yes,' the one with a blonde ponytail replied. 'Are you?'

'Yes, but I've no idea where I'm going.'

'We've got to go to the hall to register. Our new teachers will take us to the classrooms from there.'

'Thanks,' she felt relieved. 'I'll follow you then.'

The four girls trooped into the big school hall and waited in a mass of nervous, excited chatter until their names were called and they lined up behind their new teacher.

Sandra Thorpe had spent the entire morning tutting, as she went through the house tweaking a curtain here, adjusting a chair there. As soon as her husband and daughter had left, she began checking the rooms and making sure everything was just so. She had decided to put the coffee table in front of the living room window (or did lounge sound posher?), but knew that would annoy Louise, as it would restrict her tumbling space somewhat. Oh well, she had a big garden with a long stretch of grass to train on and she was thinking of buying her one of those eight-foot-long practice beams. She'd be fine.

She had set up the ironing board in the corner of the dining room and began going through her pile. Ironing was the chore she both loved and hated the most. She chose to iron absolutely everything – dolls' clothes, underwear, even her husband's horrible cotton handkerchiefs that she had to boil wash in the saucepan once a week. She would spend a good hour ironing, at least, so she had plenty to moan about once her family were back in the house.

Later, after her ironing was finished, she had just sat down with a cup of weak coffee when the doorbell rang. Lady Olga made a poor effort at a bark. 'You're never going to make a guard dog, girl, I just wouldn't bother trying!'

At the door, there was a woman maybe four or five years older than her, with short dark hair and big glasses like Deidre Barlow from *Coronation Street.* She was holding a big homemade cake on a cake stand. 'Hi,' she said, proffering the food. 'I'm Chloe Smallacre. We've just got back from holiday, or I would have been round earlier. We've been in France for two weeks. We go with the Village Twinning Group; you'll have to join. We had a week at our twinned village then stayed in Paris for a week. Have you been?' Without waiting for an answer, Chloe marched uninvited into the hallway and through to the front room.

'No, I haven't. Oh, I'm Sandra!' she said, unheard by the brazen arrival as she steamed past.

'Oh, I like how you've done it. The Greens were very old-fashioned in their furniture tastes, it felt a bit like walking into a museum at times.'

Sandra walked through into the kitchen and placed the cake down gingerly on the side.

'Tea, please, if you're making one,' came a voice from the sofa. 'White, two sugars.'

Raising her eyebrows to the ceiling, she put the kettle on before going back through to see Lady Olga tarting herself, on her back having her tummy tickled. Oh well, at least one of them was happy to have someone new come round to visit.

Mr. Thorpe got home at 5:30pm. As he pulled into the driveway, he nearly ran over a strange woman he'd never seen before. He parked, got out and was met with a thrust-out hand to shake and a woman telling him lots of facts, the only one of which went in was that her name was Chloe.

'Robert,' he said. 'Rob.'

She waved at his wife and crossed over the road, opening the front door of number seven.

'Oh,' he said, in his most depressed voice. 'She lives near us.'

'Yes, and you haven't had to listen to her for the last umpteen hours. I have heard her entire life story. Twice!'

'Great!'

'She did bring cake though.'

Louise ran downstairs in her tracksuit. 'Hi love!'' he greeted her.

She kept on moving. 'Hi Dad!'

'First day good?'

'Yep.'

She went through the kitchen and out into the garden.

'Training,' explained Sandra. She sighed. 'Suppose I'd better put the tea on. I'm late now, thanks to the neighbour from hell.'

Louise briefly popped back to get her trainers. 'Bit cold for gym shoes out there.'

'Oh love,' he stopped her. 'I interviewed Tom O'Connor today.'

'Oh, that's nice.' She was gone again.

He walked into the kitchen and put the kettle on for a much-needed cup of tea.

'I interviewed Tom O'Connor today.' He was a journalist at the regional newspaper and always talking to interesting people.

His wife ignored him. 'I've done all your ironing for you. I'll put it away later. Hurry up and get your drink, so I've got the whole kitchen to cook in.'

He did as he was told, taking his cuppa into the lounge, and sitting on the sofa. The dog and cat both jumped up after him, snuggling themselves into either side. He took turns stroking them. 'I interviewed Tom O'Connor today,' he told them.

'Meow!' said Mitty.

'Well at least someone's interested.'

Chloe couldn't wait till her husband Gerry got in from supermarket shopping. She'd sent him off to do that, while she unpacked their suitcases and started getting through the vast amount of post-holiday washing, drying and ironing.

'I met the new neighbours!' she said, as Gerry struggled through the door with twenty carrier bags.

He was only interested in kicking his shoes off and sitting down with a beer. It had been a long day. But he knew Chloe wouldn't shut up, so she prepared himself for the earache, smiling and saying, 'Oh, yes?' as she waited for his response with anticipation.

'I had a good chat with the woman – Sandra. Briefly saw her husband, just to say hi to, he's called Rob. They're a few years younger than us. The daughter flew past, she's a gymnast. They used to live in the city, near the West Common. Got a nice cat and a dog, some kind of spaniel with floppy ears.'

Gerry looked at their three snappy little Chihuahuas and wished they'd bought spaniels instead. You could sit a spaniel on your lap and stroke it without getting your finger bitten off.

'Hmm, that's nice..'

She still hadn't stopped talking, but he'd managed to blank out a few minutes of it. Hopefully he wouldn't have to answer a quiz on it later.

'I told them they should join the Twinning Committee and come with us to France.'

'We've only just got back from France!'

'Well, yes, it's not until next year now anyway, but it'd be nice to have some fresh faces on the committee. Instead of all those old blokes.'

He could understand that; the average age of the committee must be eighty-odd, and they were all very set in their ways. Some youngster had once suggested they could do trips to Germany instead of always going to France. They'd been shot down straight away – not literally, but almost. As they left the village hall, they could still hear shouts of 'Traitor!' following them. The War was still a big part of the Village Twinning Committee.

The following week, Louise told her dad she didn't need any more embarrassing lifts to school, because she was going to be walking up with Jayne.

'Who's Jayne?' he asked.

'Jayne Stewart! My best friend!'

Her parents exchanged questioning eyebrow expressions. It seemed Jayne was news to both of them.

'We sat next to each other in class from the first day, I must have mentioned her?'

'The only girls I've heard you talk about recently have been Olga Korbut and Nadia Comaneci!'

'Mmm, fair point, Mum. Miss Hill sat us together and she's fab. Anyway, she's new here like me, so she didn't know anyone either.'

'Where's she from?'

'Cambridge.'

'Ooh, nice.' Said her mother.

'Does she do gymnastics?' asked her father.

'Oh yes!' she laughed. 'We want to try to get into the school team together. She can already do a free walkover, so she must be good.'

'Well, it's nice you've made a friend. Where are you meeting her?'

'At the village green. She lives on that new estate you were on about, the one they're still building.'

'Ooh, her dad must have a good job then,' said her mum. That kind of thing was important to Sandra.

'I'll ask her!' replied her daughter, winking at her dad. She grabbed an apple, walking out the door with her school bag and her P.E. kit. It was Double Games today, which she was looking forward to.

'See ya later!' she shouted behind her.

She met up with Jayne as planned and they walked towards the school chatting about walkovers, back flips and free cartwheels. They were both sporty and were pleased they had Double Games, even though they weren't sure what they would be doing. They'd had so much information thrown at them; they were both a bit confused. They had Homework Diaries in a dull beige, with timetables stuck into the front, so they knew which subject they were studying, when and where, but it was still all very new. At least if they got lost, they'd get lost together, as the whole class stayed as one, they weren't put in sets until later on.

They sat next to each other from the first morning, but both Louise and Jayne were shy and hadn't had the courage to do more than exchange smiles. It was only when Louise noticed Jayne doodling a gymnast on her Homework Diary that she'd piped up with 'That looks like Shaposhnikova doing her planche on beam!' It turned out that was exactly what the drawing represented and then they were chatting about the 1980 Olympics and the USSR team so much, Miss Hall had to tell them to be a bit quieter – though not in a stern way, she seemed pleased the two new girls had made friends with each other and discovered something in common.

At break time, they were chatting about their fellow classmates, who they were slowly getting to know. One of them, Sabrina, was especially distinctive. She was the oldest in their class, having turned twelve just after the school year started, but she had already been told off for wearing make-up and big hooped earrings. She even had a boyfriend, two years older than her, called Paul. Louise and Jayne were too wrapped up in gymnastics to bother much about boys and thought it was funny that Sabrina and Paul seemed so loved up. They even snogged in corners of the playground, which Louise and Jayne thought was quite disgusting!

The following Monday, Sandra walked the dog up to the shops and back, enjoying the quiet of the village and being impressed how everyone said hello or acknowledged her. Several people stopped to pat Lady Olga, of course, with her long wavy ears and big brown eyes. She was always an attraction.

On the way back, Sandra had a look at the village hall notice board to see what was coming up. There seemed to be a lot on. She was too old for Mothers and Toddlers (or at least Louise was!) and too young for the Bridge Club she thought, shivering. Ditto the Gardening Club and Women's Institute. But there was a book club on Thursday nights, maybe she'd give that a whirl? Being a housewife and not required to do the school run anymore, she was finding it a bit hard to make friends. It had been so easy where she used to live, a whole load of mums bonding over their little darlings (or little shits, depending!) and chatting at the school gates. They would meet up at each other's houses for coffee and birthday parties for them and their kids. It had been quite a nice little gang. She knew they were only seven miles away, but sometimes it seemed like they were seven hours away, especially when none of the mums could drive. No, she needed to make new friends here and a book club sounded a good idea.

She was deep in thought as she walked into the cul-de-sac, so didn't notice Chloe standing outside her house until she was right in front of her. There was no escape, she had to invite her in.

Damn. Chloe took charge of the dog, taking her lead off and making a big fuss of her, while Sandra went through to the kitchen.

'Tea or coffee?' she shouted through, murmuring 'or arsenic?' under her breath.

'Coffee please, love, white, two sugars.'

Sandra pulled her face from a grimace to a smile as she walked through into the front room, carrying the two cups. Chloe was sat on the sofa with the dog (who was shamelessly on her back again, accepting tickle tums) so Sandra sat on the armchair furthest away, placing her drink on the coaster nearby.

'Had a nice day, San?'

'Dra!' she added. She abhorred her name being shortened.

Oblivious to the annoyance of her hostess, Chloe continued unabashed. 'I popped round to tell you about our little soirée we're having. Our Alfred is coming home soon, he's been away in the Navy fighting for our country.' (Sandra was expecting her to stand up and sing the National Anthem any minute now, while pulling a Union Jack out of her arse.)

'Oh yes,' replied Sandra. Her old Drama teacher would be so impressed with her. That almost sounded like she gave a damn! 'Alfred? How old is he?'

'Twenty-two. We named him after my father.' (Lucky boy, thought Sandra sarcastically.)

'So, on Saturday evening,' Chloe went on, 'we're having a big Welcome Home do and of course you're all invited. It'll be amazing! Fizz and nibbles and something decent on the stereo, you'll love it.'

Sandra wasn't so sure about that. She was desperately trying to think of something they could be doing that evening, which would prevent them from going.

'Rob might be working late that night.' It was the best she could come up with at short notice.

'Oh, that's fine, you and Louise come over early, Rob can join you later. It'll be going all evening. We thought from about five o'clock onwards.' (God, she was indefatigable! thought Sandra.) She continued 'All the neighbours are invited, so no one will complain. Oh, except for Nora No-Mates at number thirteen. No one wants Nora at your party and if she complains, no one will listen anyway. The police and the council have got her blacklisted as a nuisance caller.'

Sandra hadn't met the delightful Nora yet, but her reputation had preceded her, and it wasn't at the top of her agenda.

'Okay, I'll just check with Louise and Rob, but I'm sure we can at least pop over at some point.'

'And if you don't, I'll just get Gerry to come and drag you across the road!' She was laughing, but Sandra believed her. This woman was a force of nature.

Sandra stood up to take the cups through. 'Well Louise will be home from school soon, so I'd better think about getting the tea on.'

'Oh, don't be silly, we've a while yet. Put the kettle on, I'll have another.'

Sandra returned to the kitchen, taking deep breaths. Maybe Nora wasn't the worst person in the cul-de-sac? At least she hadn't been round to bother them so far. She'd done a lot of peering round curtains though. It felt a bit like being stalked every time she took the dog out, the old-fashioned floral curtains doing more than twitching as she walked past.

When Rob and Louise got home, they were about as excited about the soirée as Sandra was.

'Fizz and nibbles, mind!' she teased. They both rolled their eyes at the same time.

'I'll guess we'll have to put in an appearance at any rate,' grumbled Robert, sitting down with a cup of tea and the cat.

'Perhaps I can develop a headache or something?' Louise chipped in.

'She'd still expect us to go,' moaned her mother.

'Could I bring Jayne, do you think?'

Sandra shrugged. 'Probably. She reckons most of the village are going anyway.'

'I suppose it's a good opportunity to meet the rest of the neighbours,' Robert piped up. He always tried to see the positive in everything. 'You might make some more friends, Sandra.'

'I haven't made any yet! You really can't count Chloe as a friend. More of an unwanted house invader! A bit like fleas!' They giggled at her, as she continued. 'Anyway, I have a plan to meet nicer people - normal people!' They looked up at her with interest. 'There's a book club at the village hall on Thursday evenings. I thought I'd give it a look over.'

'Can I come?'

'I'm not sure actually, Louise, it didn't say any age limit, but you do love your books. I'll go on my own this week and let you know what it's like. I might be the youngest one there!'

Louise had a day off from Chloe the next day, thankfully, but in hindsight, she probably would have preferred a repeat visit from her.

The doorbell was being rang for the second time in a few seconds. 'Bloody hell, can't even have a wee in peace!' She washed her hands quickly and got to the front door just as the bell was being pushed for a third time. She was about to say something insulting about the caller having zero patience when she noticed it was Nosy Nora and the old woman was carrying Mitty!

'Is this your cat?' she asked, before Sandra could find her own words.

'Yes, it has our phone number on his tag.' She pointed to the bright blue collar.

'You expect me to see that tiny writing? At my age? I'm 76, you know!'

'So are a lot of people, but they've got more manners than you have!'

Nora huffed and drew herself up to her full four feet ten inches. She did love a good argument.

'Well, your cat' (dragging the 'your' out to an impressive three syllables) has just done its business all over my front garden.'

She was obviously expecting more of an answer than the shrug she received. She huffed again, louder this time. 'So, what are you going to do about it?

'Nothing. Cats do that. They poo, it's normal.'

Nora took a physical step backwards, as if literally rocked by surprise and horror. Sandra took the opportunity to snatch Mitty from her arms and place her in the front room, shutting the door behind her so she couldn't get out.

'Now, Nora,' she spoke firmly, noting the woman's shock. 'Yes, I know your name, I've heard all about you and your antics. If I was you, I'd go home, leave the shit on the garden, it's great fertilizer and go inside, find some knitting and do that.' She turned to go, then thought better of it and turned back. 'And stop staring out your bloody curtains at everyone! Have you got no life?'

With that parting shot, she slammed the door and locked it behind her.

As she went back into the lounge and gave Mitty a cuddle (To be honest, he didn't seem particularly traumatized by his ordeal), she saw Nora slink off back to her house.

'And good riddance!' she shouted in her general direction. 'Bloody hell! What kind of a village have we moved into?'

Louise was having a much better time of things. Her and Jayne pretty much skipped the way home with their exciting news. They agreed to talk to each other on the phone after telling their parents.

Louise dashed in to find her mother ironing another vast mountain.

'Mum! Mum! Guess what? Mrs. Leighton has said that me and Jayne should try to get into the City Gymnastics Club. She says we're the best in the year and they are looking for pre-teens to start training.'

'Wow! Slow down!' said her mum, giving her a hug. 'How exciting!'

'The trials are on Fridays at six o'clock. Can we go, Mum? Can we? Can we?'

'Hang on. Let's talk about it practically first. If you get in, how often will you need to train?'

'I think it starts off twice a week, then maybe three times and later at weekends, if you improve and get into the competitive squad.'

'Well, you know I don't drive and I'm not sure your dad would want to commit to all those trips in and out the city.'

'Jayne and I were thinking her dad and my dad could do it between them, so it wouldn't be so bad? Like her dad takes and mine brings back or something? Her dad's a postman so he's back earlier.'

'Hmm, maybe. Let's wait till your dad gets in and discuss it with him.'

'But I said I'd ring her back and let her know!'

'Well, you can just wait a bit, there's nothing to let her know yet, is there?'

Louise was pretty much jumping up and down in excitement and frustration. Her mother tried to calm her. 'Look, as soon as Dad gets in, we'll talk to him. Go and get your leo and tracksuit on and do a bit of tumbling in the garden while you're waiting. It's nice and dry out there and not too cold.'

She knew soon it would be colder weather and she'd have to accept her front room and dining room being used as a floor exercise mat, but the longer Louise could practice outside the better, thought her mother. At least going to the City Gym Club might save her carpets some wear!

It felt like a very long time for Louise to wait, but finally her dad got home, they had the conversation and he agreed to sharing the driving duties with Jayne's father, if both girls got through the trails.

'Where are you going?'

'To ring Jayne, Dad, let her know.'

He checked his watch. 'Not yet! Five to six. You know it's cheaper after six.'

'Yes, but -'

'When you pay the bills….'

'I can make the rules. Yes, I know.'

They both counted down until it was six o'clock, then she picked up the receiver and began to dial Jayne's number, watching the dial go round painfully slowly as each number clicked in.

After all the excitement, it was only later that Robert realised he hadn't told his family his own news. 'Oh, I'm interviewing Margaret Thatcher on the phone next week.'

Sandra was washing up after tea and Louise was devouring every page of the latest issue of *The Gymnast* magazine. They made some kind of half-hearted acknowledgement noises in unison.

'I've had quite a few high-profile interviews lately.'

'Hmm?'

'Yes – the Pope, the Queen, Cleopatra and Hitler.'

'That's nice,' commented his wife, putting some mugs away in the cupboard.

'Who was the nicest?' asked Louise, turning over another page and admiring a pull-out poster of Nelli Kim.

'Oh, definitely Hitler. He was a real charmer.'

'Ooh. Lovely.'

He shook his head and opened the latest copy of *World's Fair*. If you can't beat 'em...

Thursday night was Sandra's first foray into the village Book Club. The announcement on the noticeboard had said 'New Members Always Welcome' so she assumed she could just turn up. The village hall was only a couple of minutes' walk from their house, so she was there in good time. She had very little idea of what to expect, so was dressed the smart end of casual with a bit of natural looking make-up on. She put a notepad and pen in her bag in case she needed to write anything down. She liked to be prepared.

There were already some people there, chairs had been set out in quite a big circle and she could see two women through the serving hatch who were making tea and coffee in the little kitchen. She hovered nervously near the chairs and waited to be noticed. She was usually quite a confident woman, but wasn't keen on these kinds of occasions where she knew no one and wasn't completely sure what would happen.

It wasn't long before two men came in together, followed not far behind by two women and it was these that began talking to her, so she soon felt a bit more relaxed. They sat on the chairs, one either side of her and introduced themselves. Ruth was mid-forties, very sweet, warm and friendly. Brenda was a bit older, quieter and a much larger build than her slim friend. Sandra found them easy to chat to. Just as she was going to ask how the book club worked, a tall woman with her hair pulled up tightly in a bun clapped her hands together and everyone went silent.

'Hi,' she said. 'Lovely to see so many of you here this week. I'm Belinda Barber, I organize the book club, though it's really a group thing. I see a couple of new faces tonight, so welcome to you' (She indicated Sandra and a man in his seventies) 'and great to see Beryl back. Are you feeling better, love?'

'Yes, thanks.'

'Excellent. So, for those newbies, at the start of each month, we have a shortlist of books which one member introduces. We then have a vote to see which book we read, ready to discuss them next month. We have meetings every week. The first part of the evening, we discuss the books we've been reading, then we break for refreshments, then come back to the circle to discuss and chat more. If you can put 30p in the tin near the kitchen, that covers the cost of the tea, coffee and biscuits.'

Lucky I brought my purse, thought Sandra.

Belinda continued. 'So, our book this month was *1984* by George Orwell. How many of us managed to read it?'

A show of hands indicated almost everyone had.

'Sorry,' said one of the older men. 'Not had the best of health this month, my eyes have been playing up and the print was a bit small.'

'Never mind, Henry, hopefully you'll feel better this month and we can find you a large print book.'

'Thanks, love.'

'Anyway, who wants to start us off with their views on *1984*? Pauline? Excellent.'

A red-headed woman with big glasses on stood up and started to speak.

Sandra got home two hours later. Robert was sitting down with a cup of tea, stroking the dog and watching cricket on the telly. 'Oh, how was it, love?'

'Really good. I've made a couple of friends already, and it was fun.'

'Were there many people there?'

'There were actually, maybe fifteen or so. A few men as well as women.'

'Oh, it's not my kind of thing.'

Louise ran down from her bedroom. 'Did you ask if I could go?'

'I didn't, but to be honest, I don't think you'd get much out of it. I am one of the youngest, as I thought I might be. There are a lot of OAPs there. Maybe you should see if you can start one up at school? Or they might already have one?'

'Yeah, good idea, I'll ask Miss Hill tomorrow.'

In the end, Louise forgot all about book clubs the next day. It was the day of their trial at City Gymnastics Club, so all her and Jayne could think about was that. Mrs. Leighton, their P.E. teacher, had arranged for them to have an extra practice session in the lunch hour, so she could give them some final advice. They were excited and nervous in equal measure, but Mrs. Leighton reassured them that they were definitely good enough. 'I wouldn't have suggested you going for the trial otherwise, girls, you'll be great!'

By half past five, Louise was all dressed and ready to go – wearing her favourite red, white and blue Carita House leotard and a red tracksuit with white piping, which reminded her of the USSR ones. She had her hair up in a ponytail like Nadia Comaneci in 1976 and she was unable to keep still, walking between the front door and the front room window.

Finally, Jayne's father's car appeared, and she ran to it, shouting a quick 'Goodbye!' as she left, her parents wishing her a final 'Good luck!' She got in the back seat next to Jayne. She said a quick hello to her father, then the girls chatted non-stop about the trial until they got there.

They went through into the big sports hall which looked like a dream to the two young girls. Their school only had basic equipment, but City Gymnastics Club had everything, even a proper set of asymmetric bars! Neither Louise nor Jayne had ever been on the bars, they must be an expensive piece of equipment! They were in awe.

The coach came over to meet them and introduced himself as Mr. Barber. He looked a bit older than their dads and was quite stocky, they would feel safe if they were trying to somersault and needed him to catch them mid-air. Jayne's dad left them to it, wishing them more good luck as they began warming up for the trial.

The girls began on the floor exercise and both of them were confident on that piece, as it was the easiest to train. You just needed some grass, or a fairly uncluttered room and you could practice your floor routine. Louise was better at the dance side, having done ballet as a very young child and she had a natural rhythm and connected easily to the music. Jayne was better at the tumbling side and had more confidence and less fear when trying new acrobatic moves. Mr. Barber seemed very happy with them there, then took them to do a few vaults.

Next up were the bars and the girls explained they had never had the chance to go on this apparatus before. He got one of the older girls to demonstrate a few easy moves – forward and backward circles around the low bar – and the girls soon picked them up, although their hands were sore. The coach advised them to buy some handguards to protect their palms from ripping. He was then called over by the assistant coach, so the girls were left alone for a few minutes.

'Do you think that means he wants us in his club?'

'The handguards comment? Yes, I wondered the same thing.'

'Well, that's the worst thing done, bars. Just beam to go and we both train on that in school.'

'Yes, but the one at school isn't as high as this one.'

Mr. Barber came back over to them and asked each girl to do a bit of a beam routine.

'Just make something up, show me what you can do, that kind of thing.'

Louise did this all the time, she was always doing beam routines on anything she saw – low walls (like the one in her old back yard), the edge of rugs, anything that had a straight line and was about four inches wide. So, this was fun for her, even though she was very aware this beam was at full competition height, and it did make her split leaps a bit more cautious.

Jayne wasn't really into making up routines, preferring to learn new skills, but she showed her best moves and didn't fall off, so she was happy.

It turned out the coach was too. They went into his office, discussed a few options for which classes they could get to, then were given a list of rules and a place to buy the green club leotard and tracksuit from.

By then, it was seven o'clock and Louise's dad turned up to collect them. He was briefed by Mr. Barber too, then they shook hands and the three of them walked to the car. The girls were absolutely ecstatic, they couldn't stop talking, going over everything they had seen and done.

Rob was thinking more of the practical side of things. 'So how many times a week are we going to be ferrying our little gymnasts about then?'

They still hadn't come down from all the excitement of the trial at gym club when it was soon time to get ready for Alfred's Welcome Home party the next day. Despite the family's initial reluctance to go, they were all quite looking forward to it now. Louise was just happy because Jayne was going with her, and it meant they were allowed to dress up and wear a bit of make-up. Rob was hoping he might meet some more of the local men and maybe make a pal or two. Sandra was most excited about getting to have a nosy round Chloe and Gerry's house and see what it was like inside!

Chloe had said to go over anytime from five, but Sandra didn't want to appear too keen, so they agreed to saunter over at half past six. They kept reminding themselves that it was literally only over the road, if they wanted to go home early.

They walked in through the open front door, Chloe rushing over to them, greeting them as if they were her best friends who'd been lost in a snowstorm and had only just reappeared. She introduced everyone in a flurry of names which no one would remember, indicated where the food and drink were, then flew off to greet the next guests to arrive.

'At least it looks like she'll be too busy to chat!' whispered Sandra to her husband. The girls had already made a beeline for the crisps and lemonade and were giggling over something in the back garden, where other party guests were standing in little groups.

Sarah from number five saw them and gave them a cheery wave, which they returned.

After a few minutes, a man of about fifty came over to say hello, average height, maybe slightly overweight but with a twinkle in his eye. He introduced himself as Hugh and said he lived next door but one to the Smallacres. Sandra remembered spotting him on one of her dog walks. 'Oh, you've got the two black Labradors?'

'Yes, that's right, Sooty and Sweep. And you've got the little spaniel.'

They chatted dogs for a couple of minutes, then Hugh excused himself.

Chloe's husband Gerry came over to introduce himself, as he hadn't met the Thorpes yet, though had heard plenty about them from his wife, of course. Sandra thought what a lovely man he was and felt great sympathy for him having to live with the *tour de force* that was Chloe. Then she heard someone call her name and left Robert and Gerry talking about cricket.

It was Ruth and Brenda from the village book club. She was pleased to see them; they had been so welcoming and friendly the other night. She explained how she knew Chloe, pointing out their house through the front window. It turned out the two women lived round the corner, on the same estate but the street behind this one. As they said that, Sandra suddenly had a lightbulb moment and thought they might be a couple but didn't like to ask. I mean, what on earth would you say? She guessed she'd find out in time anyway.

The Smallacre's heap of chihuahuas were snuggled in their cages, occasionally snarling menacingly if an ankle came too close. The women were admiring them in the same way you do a tiger at the zoo, being quite relieved they were behind bars.

'We've got three cats,' explained Brenda. 'Rod, Jane and Freddy!'

Ruth giggled. 'My daughter Bryony used to love watching *Rainbow*.'

'Oh yes,' recalled Sandra. 'Zippy and Bungle!'

'Yes, those were our other cats, but we sadly lost them over the last few years.'

'But we still have our lovely three kitties. Do you have any pets, Sandra?'

'Oh yes, we've got a black and white cat called Mitty and a Cavalier King Charles Spaniel dog called Lady Olga.'

In the garden, Louise and Jayne were giggling away, plotting to try some of the wine that people were leaving on tables, as they handily deposited their pretty glasses on the patio tables before wandering off and forgetting about them.

'It'll be easier when it's darker out here and no one can see us,' Louise whispered.

The garden was decorated with multi-coloured lights fitted around the trees and fencing, but there was a dark area at the back that seemed to be a small flower bed. It was directly behind the garage so was naturally in shadow.

'Let's see if we can nick some glasses and store them back there until later.'

Jayne nodded conspiratorially and that's what they did. When glasses were left, and the adults nipped into the house for food or the loo or whatever, the girls would quickly transfer them to the back bit of the garden. No one seemed to notice. If anyone came out for them later, they just assumed they'd been tidied away and got themselves another fresh glass of whatever they were drinking.

Gerry and Robert were getting on very well. They both had domineering wives, but were quiet, mild-mannered and low maintenance themselves, so they clicked straightaway and soon found plenty in common. They were currently discussing how brilliant disaster movies were and debating whether *The Poseidon Adventure* was better than *The Towering Inferno*.

Suddenly Chloe clinked her glass with a spoon. 'Quick everyone! Be quiet. Alfred's just at the top of the cul-de-sac. I want you all to give him a big cheer when he gets in!'

The word went out to the back garden too and everyone came through to see the prodigal son come home after his long time overseas with the Navy. The party wasn't a surprise, but his mother had invited all her friends, so it took him a while to pick out the faces of people he actually knew!

His mother put the record player on and the strains of Peters and Lee singing *Welcome Home* rang out across the room. Once it had finished, there was another cheer, a quick toast – Alfred was handed a glass of something alcoholic from the hand of someone he didn't know – then the party continued as before.

He was introduced to the new neighbours who both found him polite and charming. Rob stayed chatting to Gerry, while Sandra took Alfred into the garden to find Louise. The girls were giggling near a tree, so she called them over and did the introductions. Her job done, she went back inside looking for more wine and Ruth and Brenda to talk to.

Louise and Jayne meanwhile were left open-mouthed and speechless.

'My God, he's gorgeous!' Jayne managed, eventually.

Louise nodded. 'Isn't he! Wow!'

Alfred was literally tall, dark and handsome. He was slim, but looked fit and strong, not weedy. He had his hair cut short in that Navy style. 'Call me Alfie!' he'd said to them, when Sandra brought him over. The girls hadn't been able to muster up any words, just vague smiles and he'd soon wandered off and was talking with another couple.

Still in a bit of a swoon, Louise and Jayne decided now was a good time to go to their stash of glasses and sample their first wine, or was it champagne? Who knew? Clear and fizzy stuff in pretty posh glasses anyway. It was surprisingly easy to drink, it had a light taste and they liked it.

'Bit like lemonade,' reviewed Jayne.

Louise agreed and they drank the rest of it easily.

Sandra excused herself from her new book club buddies and found her husband, drinking whisky with his new best friend Gerry.

'Should we be getting going soon? It's half past nine. I'm not sure what time Jayne's parents are expecting her?'

'Oh, I think she said she was allowed to stay over, as it's not a school night.'

'Okay, shall I go and round them up though? Don't want to leave the dog too long either.'

Rob nodded, resignedly. 'Gotta do what the old woman says, eh?' he whispered to Gerry, who agreed with lots of empathy.

Sandra soon reappeared, running and a bit breathless. 'Rob! Quick! It's the girls!'

'What's wrong?' He stood up, as did Gerry (albeit slightly unsteadily, as they'd had a few whiskies) and they followed her outside.

Louise and Jayne were sat on the floor, their heads resting on each other and sleeping peacefully. Surrounding them were more than a dozen empty wine glasses.

'Oops!' said Gerry. 'Do you want a hand getting these two back to yours?'

The next morning, Sandra rang Jayne's mum asking if it was okay for her to stay for lunch, to which she agreed. She had her hands full with Jayne's two-year-old brother anyway, who was shrieking in the background, due to teething.

Sandra put the phone down and turned to the two girls. 'Right, I've bought you some time, Jayne. Take a paracetamol, both of you and drink lots of water. I will not be covering for you again, so I hope you have both learnt your lesson.' They nodded, heads down, feeling ashamed. 'I'll make you some toast, then when you've had that and your medication, you can both take Lady Olga for a walk round the estate.'

More sheepish nodding.

'And, Louise, it's your birthday very soon, so if you want any kind of celebration whatsoever, I expect you to be on your best behaviour from now on!'

The girls did as they were told and an hour later, they were feeling a lot less delicate as they took the dog out. They were both rather subdued though.

'I did enjoy it overall,' said Jayne, though she sounded like she was trying to convince herself as much as her friend.

'That Alfie's a right dish!'

'Isn't he just?'

'Shame he's so much older than us.'

'But still nice to look at!' They giggled in agreement.

As they walked round the street behind theirs, they saw Ruth and Brenda coming out from one of the front doors.

'Hello girls! Did you enjoy the party?'

'Yes thanks,' they replied politely in unison. 'Did you?'

'Oh yes,' Brenda said. 'Your mum is so lovely, really easy to talk to.'

'Yes,' agreed Ruth. 'We're pleased she decided to join the book club.'

Louise smiled. 'Yes, she's really glad she did too. She says it's quite hard to make friends once you stop doing the school runs.'

Olga started pulling towards the grass, so they moved on, waving at the two women.

'Mum said they lived together. They must be best friends.'

'Yes,' agreed Jayne. 'Maybe we'll live together when we're older?'

'With a million cats, all named after famous gymnasts?'

As they rounded the next corner, they both gasped as they almost walked straight into Alfred.

'Oh God, sorry,' he said, 'I wasn't looking where I was going. What a gorgeous dog!'

He knelt down to stroke her back and the red wavy fur of her ears. 'I love Cavaliers, so much friendlier than our evil Chihuahuas!'

'She's called Lady Olga,' Louise finally managed to say something.

'Nice name. Well, I'd better get on. Mum's sent me to the shops for bin bags, we're still tidying up after the party. See you later, girls! And Lady Olga!'

He walked away, luckily not turning back. If he had done, he would have seen two open-mouthed schoolgirls looking at him like he was a pop star!

They walked back to the house in silence.

October 1981

Rob knocked on Gerry's door at seven o'clock in the evening.

'Hey Gerry, I'm all on my lonesome for once. Fancy sneaking out to the pub for a quick beer?'

'Ooh yes, I can. Chloe will be fine with Alfred here. Where are your lot tonight?'

'Well, Sandra's at Book Club and Louise is at gymnastics training, and they don't finish until nine. Plus, Jayne's dad is picking them up, so I don't have a curfew!'

'Excellent. Hang on a min.'

Gerry disappeared and Rob could hear him talking to Chloe. He returned with his jacket and wallet, and they set off out together. It was a cold, but dry, evening and only about a ten-minute walk to the pub. They passed the village hall on the way, Gerry teasing Rob that he could choose to join Sandra at Book Club if he preferred.

'I'll decline your kind suggestion! As much as I enjoy reading, I prefer to do it when I want and read what I want and not have to discuss my thoughts with a room full of people.'

'Yeah, fair enough. And – no beer!'

'Exactly.'

They continued up the road. It was the main road through the village, it went all the way up to the school and beyond one way, or down to the next village the other. This time of night, it was quiet though. Most people were settled at home, eating tea, watching telly, relaxing after school or work. They could see the lights shining through the windows of the houses they walked past, the odd flicker of a TV screen.

The pub was pretty much opposite the village green. It was in two sections – one part where the younger people tended to go, those who wanted loud music and socializing. Then there was the smaller section at the back where the old men went to have their pints and chat about the racing. Although Gerry and Rob were much younger than the old boys there, they both headed straight for that part. They wanted to chat at a reasonable level and to be able to hear each other; they didn't want all the noise and chaos of the bigger bit.

There wasn't a queue here either, which was another advantage. Geoff said hello to a couple of men he vaguely knew, then him and Rob went to sit in the corner with their drinks.

'What's it like having Alfred back home?'

'Oh it's great. Chloe always worries when he's off away somewhere.'

'Well, that's natural. Mothers are bad at that. Or good at it – whichever way you look at it! Born worriers. My mother's the same.'

'Mine was too. No, it's lovely having him home. Sometimes I just wish he could get a normal job and still live with us.'

'Does he love being in the Navy?'

'I don't know. I think it's more of a job than a vocation. He has talked about leaving and doing something else.'

'And Chloe would prefer that, I guess?'

'Definitely! Me too. In fact, I've been thinking about talking to him later in the year, see if he'd consider moving back in with us.'

'How long is he staying this time?'

'Oh not long, probably. Sometimes it's a week, sometimes a month, four months. We never know. He can get called up at any time and have to go pretty much straight away.'

'Must be hard to plan anything.'

'Exactly. That's why we had the Welcome Home party for him. We don't know if he'll be here for his birthday, Christmas, New Year. So we party when we can!'

'Good idea! Just next time you have one, we'll ban Louise and Jayne from coming!' He laughed and rolled his eyes.

'Maybe they learnt a lesson?'

'Hmm, maybe. But let's face it, it won't be the last time they get drunk, will it?'

'I'll drink to that!'

Their first beer already finished, Rob went to the bar to order them both a second. It was nice having this bit of freedom, where he didn't have to be Dad or Husband, he could just be Rob. He was sure Gerry felt the same too. Sometimes a bit of male company was exactly what they needed.

It was October 23rd and Louise's twelfth birthday. She had been asked if she wanted either a big party and a small present, or a small party and a big present. She chose the latter. So, Jayne was coming over for a birthday lunch. Sandra already had everything prepared and laid out on the dining table, covered in cling film to keep it all fresh. There were little sandwiches cut into triangles with the crusts cut off (because Sandra had been told that was how posh people did them), sausage rolls, a big bowl of salad (which the girls were unlikely to touch), small bowls of different flavours of crisps and Louise's favourite party snacks – cheese and pineapple on sticks.

But first, it was time to open her birthday cards which had come in the post and the presents from her parents. The first gift she unwrapped was a blue and white leotard with stars on. She recognized the design immediately. 'It's the one Nadia Comaneci wore this year in the display in America!'

'Yes, that's right, I saw you admiring the leotard in *The Gymnast* magazine, so I ordered it when you weren't looking.'

'Oh thanks, Mum, that's just perfect.'

The other presents from her mum and dad were a new pair of gym slippers and handguards (the ones her coach had recommended), plus a set of books by Noel Streatfeild. She loved everything and was already very happy and excited to try out her new gym clothes.

'There's something else,' said her dad. 'Out in the garden.'

Intrigued, she ran out into the back garden and there was a practice beam, half size length and a couple of inches off the floor, covered in a soft blue carpet. A big pink bow was tied around the middle of it.

'Oh wow!' she said, running out to it. She took the ribbon off carefully and started walking up and down it, doing little dance moves, poses and jumps.

'Why don't you have some breakfast then change out of your pyjamas, try your new leotard on and have a go on the beam for a bit before Jayne comes?'

'Could I ring her and tell her to bring a leo, so she can have a go on the beam too?'

'Go on then!'

She excitedly ran to the phone in the hall and dialled her best friend's number.

In the afternoon, Louise and her parents went into Lincoln to see her aunties, uncles and grandmothers for a big family tea. They were a family that relished a chance to get everyone together as much as possible. Louise wasn't too keen on being the centre of attention for long, but it did have its advantages, especially with the inevitable birthday cards and gifts she received. It was all very exciting!

One of her best presents was a Five-Year Diary, a small white one with a girl on the front in an old-fashioned long pink dress with a wide-brimmed flowery hat and a delicate parasol. She loved it straight away, although worried she'd be likely to lose the tiny keys needed for the lock. There was no way she was going to give her mother the spare one for safe keeping! She would be tempted to read her daughter's entries anyway, Louise had no qualms about that. Her mother's nosiness was legendary. Though Sandra said it wasn't nosiness, it was "healthy curiosity."

Louise enjoyed writing and had been thinking of keeping a diary, but wasn't sure what to do, if she should wait until the New Year and start on January 1st, or what? But now she had the answer, she could start now and had five years to fill it up. There were only four lines per day, but that would be enough for at least some brief highlights of what had happened.

That evening, she opened up the brand-new book, trying not to damage the unblemished spine. She opened it to October 23rd and filled in the year as 1981. Wow! There was space to keep filling it in up to 1985! That seemed so far away. God knows what life would be like then when it was her 16th birthday!

It was the October half term. During every half term and the school holidays, Louise would go to each of her grandparents' houses for a day or two. Her Nanna (Dad's mum) and her Grandma (Mum's mum) were both widowed and lived by themselves at either end of the same road, Nanna near the Castle, Gran near the old Army Barracks. She loved the days she spent with them and had many years of happy memories growing up with them in her life so often.

Now she was twelve, she didn't expect them to have to entertain her in the same way. When she was a bit younger, she would get them to make cut-out dolls, cutting figures of girls from catalogues or pattern books. She would then write their names on the back and play schools with them or gymnastics or Brownies or beauty competitions.

Nowadays, she'd bring a book she was reading or something she was writing. She would stick her gymnastics cuttings into scrapbooks. She would do wordsearches or puzzle books with Grandma and play Scrabble with Nanna. They would cook her favourite meal – beef stew and dumplings – and each hope their meal was the best. Gran had a piano in her front room and although Louise never had any lessons, she could read music and play by ear, so spent many hours occupying herself trying to improve her skills.

Nanna had a little Yorkshire terrier dog called Kim, so they would go out for walks and pop into the local shops, especially if it was Big Bag Shopping Day. This was the day Nanna's pension arrived, so she had to go to the Post Office to collect it and would visit all the shops along the road – the bakers, butchers, corner shop, greengrocers – to stock up on provisions. Louise liked going on these little adventures, especially when a second-hand bookshop opened two doors away from Nanna's house. She even found a Nadia Comaneci biography there for 20p!

Grandma didn't have any pets, so Louise would sometimes take Lady Olga with her, which they all enjoyed. She was a real lap dog and was happy being stroked and cuddled, so she liked sitting on Gran's knee and trying to cadge one of the broken biscuits she kept in a jar, alongside the special Rupert the Bear tissues she always had in for her only grandchild to use.

Her Grandma was sixty-four and her Nanna ten years older, but they were both fit and sprightly. Neither of them could drive, so they walked wherever they needed to go and both of them still went ballroom dancing, which they loved. These two amazing women were big influences on Louise's life, and she loved spending days with them.

Sarah Willington was enjoying her half term break from work and feeling quite content with life. She'd had a difficult couple of years previously, losing her mother and finding her fiancé had cheated on her. Moving to New Barnham had signified a big change, one she had organized and fulfilled, surprising herself with strength she didn't think she had. She looked for teaching jobs anywhere in the country and had found this one in a lovely little village hundreds of miles from everyone who knew her.

It had all tied in beautifully – the new job, the house for sale. She sold her mother's old house and used the money to set herself up in Lincolnshire. She wasn't dependent on her mother for a place to live and she wasn't dependent on her boyfriend any longer. In fact, he didn't even know where she was. He was domineering and intimidating and she wanted to leave all that behind. She had even changed her surname to her mother's maiden name. She didn't want her ex to decide he wanted to ditch his current squeeze and come looking for her. Away from the situation, she could see he was trouble.

At first she had been reticent to talk to the new people she met. She wasn't sure if she could trust anyone again. But she soon got into village life and her neighbours seemed a good bunch – apart from the nosy old woman across the road who seemed to be constantly spying. She vowed to get to know everyone better and to make more of an effort to mix in, not keep herself aloof. It was just a hard habit to break when her ex had vetted all her friends and instructed her who she could see and when. She had to get used to being able to make her own choices again.

At least her current boyfriend was completely different. He was happy to let her choose her own path and he didn't expect her to do as she was told. In fact, he appreciated her independent spirit and valued it. He was away a lot at the moment but planned to settle in the UK again soon and she secretly hoped he would move in with her. That would just complete her happiness. She saw her reflection in the hall mirror. 'Silly girl!' she scolded herself, 'look at that stupid grin. You be careful!' But she was enjoying being happy. And for God's sake, did she deserve it!

November 1981

One of Robert Thorpe's big love was circuses and that week, there was one on in Nottingham – Fossett's Circus – one of the big British circuses, so the three of them went to see it. Rob was a big kid whenever he was in the Big Top, he'd make his daughter cringe by shouting out responses to the clowns' questions.

'Audience participation,' he would say, in response to Louise's glares. 'It's what you're supposed to do.'

'Only if your age is in single figures, Dad. Stop being embarrassing.'

'Aww, leave him alone, Louise,' Sandra said, digging her husband in the ribs. 'This is how he nurtures his inner child!'

'I'm not sure it needs any more nurturing!'

Despite her protestations, and not being entirely enamoured with the clowns, Louise did enjoy watching the elegant horses trotting round the ring and the excitable circus dogs playing football with balloons. You could tell they were really enjoying themselves and they were fun to watch for that reason. She also loved watching any act which had an element of gymnastics in it – the *Corde Lisse*, tumbling acts, the high wire…

As a young, leggy girl swung into upside-down splits on the trapeze, Sandra whispered to her daughter 'You were named after a trapeze artist, you know.'

'Really?'

'Yes. I was pregnant with you and your dad dragged me –' Rob cleared his throat pointedly. 'Escorted me,' she amended, 'to a circus on the South Common. There was a really good trapeze artist, I think she was Scandinavian. Anyway, after that we both said what a lovely name Louise was, so that was it really.'

'Oh wow! I never knew that. Well, no wonder I'm a gymnast then.'

'Exactly.'

'Didn't stop me being afraid of heights though.'

'No.'

'Shh!' hissed her father.

A few minutes later, Louise asked her mum 'What was I going to be called if I was a boy?'

'Kelvin.'

'Blimey! Thank God I'm a girl. Was that a clown's name, by any chance?'

'No,' laughed her mother. 'We just liked it. We could have really named you after a clown. How about Coco? Or Sonny?'

'Hmm. Maybe not, Mum.'

After the show, they walked round outside looking at the animals. They were all in beautiful condition, though the llamas hissed a bit and didn't seem very friendly. Louise fell in love with one of the horses who was happy to let her stroke him. The lad who was looking after them told Louise the horse was called Henley.

'Oh he's lovely!' She spent several more minutes fussing him.

'Come on then,' said Rob. 'We'd better set off home.'

'And Henley won't fit in the back seat, before you ask!' advised Sandra.

On the way home, Louise was silent for a while before asking 'Maybe I could have horse riding lessons? There's a stables in the village.'

'I know there is, but it's very expensive. Plus there's the time commitment, you couldn't put 100% into both gymnastics and horse riding.'

'Hmm. I guess not. Shame though. I do like horses.'

'You're better off sticking to the vaulting horse!'

'Argh. Typical Dad and his puns!'

It was soon November 5th and Bonfire Night, the Thorpe family's first one in the village. It was quite a big event. Every year, a bonfire was organized on the village green with the chip shop conveniently nearby to provide refreshments. It seemed that nearly everyone was there, and Louise had fun spotting her classmates in the light of the huge flames. A few of the kids were waving sparklers around, but her mum didn't let her have one, after hearing on the News about a girl getting her hand severely burnt. She wasn't too fussed anyway; she was quite happy eating her chips out of paper and her mushy peas out of a little plastic tub.

Jayne wasn't around that weekend; they had gone down south to visit her grandma. Louise's dad had walked up the village with her. He was now chatting away to Gerry over chips and bottles of beer. Louise was standing slightly apart, enjoying the spectacle, watching the flames soaring and listening to the fire's crackle and spit.

'Hello!'

She turned round to see Alfie.

'Oh hi! I see our dads are chatting away.'

'Yes, new best mates!'

'Your friend not with you?'

'No, she's away.'

They looked at the bonfire, while Alfie nicked one of Louise's chips, pretending to be sneaky about it.

'I thought they'd put a guy of Nora on the bonfire,' she said. 'She seems the most unpopular person in the village.'

He didn't laugh, but said sadly 'Yes, it's a shame really. All the complaining she does – phoning the police, writing to the council and everything – it's all because she's lonely and wants attention.'

'But everyone just gets annoyed with her!'

'Well, yes, it's a bit like little kids who smack their mum. Even bad attention is attention.'

'Hmm, I guess so. Hasn't Nora got any family then?'

'No, she has, three grown up kids and some grandchildren, but they are all in different countries – the United States, Switzerland and Canada.'

'So even they can't stand to live near their mother?'

'It's sad though, isn't it? Being so alone.'

'Yes, but she just puts people's backs up, Alfie. The first time Mum met her, she came round carrying our cat, complaining he had done a poo in her garden. I mean, really, it's a cat!'

'Do you know she complained to the local police about my Welcome Home party?'

'She didn't?' Louise was shocked. 'How rude!'

'She was probably upset Mum didn't invite her. Look, I go round to see Nora sometimes, you should come too. See if you can get a new perspective of her.'

'Okay. Yeah. I'd like that.'

'Do you want a drink? I'm just going to get one from the chippy!'

'Ooh thanks, that'd be great. Lemonade please.'

'No problem.'

He went off in the direction of the chip shop. She stood there, chips going cold, feeling warm and happy with a stupid grin on her face. She couldn't wait for Jayne to come home so she could tell her friend the news. She could just imagine it. 'Alfie was at the Bonfire Night. We were chatting on our own. He bought me a drink.'

His voice broke her out of her daydreaming.

'Lemonade for the young 'un!'

She turned to take it, smiling, just about to thank him, but stopped. He was accompanied by a girl she had never seen before. She looked like a model – at least 5' 8" tall, with chest-length shiny blonde hair and super slim. She registered they were holding hands.

'This is Samantha, my fiancée.'

Louise mustered a brave smile. 'Hi, I'm Louise.'

'Sam's been in New York working. She only got back here yesterday. That's why she wasn't at my party.'

'Wow! Lovely.' Louise could feel stupid tears welling up. She looked past them and said 'Oh I've just seen my mate from school over there. I'd better go and say hi.'

'OK, see you later!'

She walked off and hid behind a tree, trying to compose herself. Stupid girl, she said. Stupid, stupid girl.

'Hi!'

Oh God, another male voice startling her. What an evening!

She wiped her eyes with the back of her hand and turned to see Tobias. He was in her class, but one of the quieter lads, so they hadn't really spoke much before.

'I thought it was you. I was trying to find people I knew. Mum and Dad have nipped into the pub.'

'Hi Tobias. My Mum's at home ironing. My dad's over there talking to our neighbour.'

'Call me Toby! How are the chips?'

She had forgotten she was carrying them. 'Cold!' she laughed, chucking them into the bin to the side of her.

'Have you seen anyone else from our class?'

'Sabrina was here earlier, but no, I haven't seen many of them. Not to really talk to anyway.'

'Some of them are quite cliquey though, aren't they? Stick with their own groups and you're lucky if they acknowledge you.'

'Yeah. It was difficult moving here and not going to primary school with any of them. Most kids already had a friendship group.'

'You're a gymnast, aren't you?'

'Yes, I just started at the City Gymnastics Club.'

'I play chess. That's my big love.'

'I play that with my dad sometimes.'

'You ought to join the chess club. Tuesday lunchtimes in the Maths classroom.'

'OK, thanks, Toby, I might well do that.'

She heard her dad calling her name and poked her head out from round the tree. 'Hi, I'm here!'

'I thought we'd walk home now. Gerry's going so we can walk together.'

'Yes, that's fine, Dad, I'll come too. Oh, this is Toby from my class.'

'Hello Toby, nice to meet you.'

'You too, Mr. Thorpe.'

'Nice chatting, Toby, see you later.' She grinned at him. It really had been nice chatting to him as well. She was much happier than she had been ten minutes earlier, when she had felt humiliated by an older man who would never have looked at her as anything but a child.

She walked home with her dad and Gerry, who were talking about the best British music groups of the 1960s. Louise kept company with her own thoughts. When they got home, her mum asked her if she'd had a good time and she replied honestly that she had. She even managed to tell her mum about meeting Alfred's girlfriend in a very neutral and unemotional way. God, being twelve was hard work sometimes though!

Sandra was really enjoying going to the book club. They seemed a lovely group of men and women and the books chosen gave her a focus in deciding what to read, something which had often put her off reading anything at all. Too much choice wasn't always a good thing! The village had a good library too, in the centre next to the supermarket, doctors and pharmacy. The chip shop was further up on the same road, the pub the other side near the newsagents and sweet shop. Sandra was familiar with all of these by now and felt pretty content with her new life and surroundings.

She sat with Ruth and Brenda at book club and once a week or so, they'd meet up for coffee at each other's houses. They had become dear friends. Hugh from number eleven went to book club too, but apart from waving at her and saying 'hi', he tended to keep himself to himself and not mix too much. Sandra wasn't quite sure what to make of him. Maybe he was shy.

This particular meeting, the usual crowd were there, and they were discussing *Jane Eyre*, when the door opened and a man they didn't know walked in, apologizing profusely for being late.

'I'm sorry, I've only just moved in, and the village hall wasn't quite where I expected it to be.'

'No problem,' said Belinda, introducing herself. 'We've not long been started. You'll soon pick it up.'

'Thanks, I'm Martin.'

There was a spare chair next to Sandra, so he sat there. She sized him up as sneakily as she could. He was about her age, dressed quite smartly, not bad looking really. When it was the refreshment break, Ruth and Brenda went off to get cups of tea, leaving Sandra to try to welcome Martin.

'Hi,' she stuck out her hand. 'Sandra. I've only been in the book club a couple of months; you'll find everyone's very nice.'

He shook her hand. 'Lovely. I only moved into the village a few months ago.'

'Oh, we did too, so my daughter could go to the school.'

'My, er, wife left me and took the house.' He was looking at the floor and nervously steepling his fingers together. 'I'm in one of the little houses up on the estate past the chippy.'

'Do you have any kids?'

'No, only a dog. At least she didn't take him!'

'Oh, what kind of dog have you got? We've got a Cavalier King Charles.'

'A Jack Russell called Scamp. He's a right handful but as loving as anything.'

'I might see you out on a dog walk then. It usually falls to me to take ours out.'

Ruth and Brenda came back then and introduced themselves to Martin, just before Belinda took centre stage again to introduce Mabel who had chosen a Charles Dickens for them to read.

'I hate Dickens!' moaned Sandra. 'I did *Bleak House* at school. It went on forever. Bloody Jarndyce and Jarndyce!'

December 1981

As November turned into December, everything was winding down towards the Christmas festivities. The kids were making more tree decorations at school than writing essays. Louise and Jayne were still training hard at gym club and had been joined by another girl from their school, Cally, who was in the year above, so they didn't really know her very well. It turned out she lived a street away from Jayne, so soon their fathers included him in the driving arrangements, and it was only one in three trips to and from gym club that they each had to do.

Cally was a really good gymnast. She was tiny, only about 4' 8" while Louise and Jayne were just under five foot. Cally looked very young for her age, but she was mature in other ways and talked about things that the younger girls didn't really understand. One evening at gym club, they arrived ten minutes before class and Cally took them round the back near some trees. She produced a packet of cigarettes and some matches and lit one for each of them. The younger girls were shocked, but Cally was quite persuasive, so they joined in and tried to smoke, copying what Cally was doing. While the thirteen-year-old made it look cool, Louise and Jayne were wheezing, coughing and spluttering all over the place. When they got into the club a few minutes later, they swilled their mouths out in the drinking fountain and took big gulps down to soothe their dry, aching throats. That was the last time either of them tried smoking.

The girls still struggled with the bars, being the piece of apparatus they had the least experience on, so the coaches tried to give them extra time to bring their skill level up to that of the girls who had been there longer. They were told that the club would be shut for two weeks over the Christmas and New Year holidays, but when they came back afterwards, they would be training for a competition against a club from Nottingham. 'So don't eat too much Christmas pud!' they were teased.

'How exciting! Our first competition!' Louise said in the car on the way home.

All three of them were excited. 'I hope I can get my tuck back somersault ready by then,' commented Cally.

Jayne added 'I just hope I can do enough moves on the bars to get a routine together!'

A couple of days later, Louise was coming home from school when Alfred came out to meet her. Thankfully this time, there was no glamorous girlfriend there to make her feel small and insignificant.

'Hey Louise, how are you?'

'Yeah, good, you?'

'Yeah. I was thinking of going over to Nora's later. As far as I know, she usually spends Christmas on her own. This year, the village hall is organizing a meal and party for people who don't have family or won't see them over the festive season, so I thought I'd go over and tell her about it, see if she wants me to put her name down.'

'That's a kind thing to do. Isn't there another elderly woman lives on her own next door to Nora? I'm sure I saw her talking to the postman the other morning.'

'Oh yes, Mabel. Her and Nora fell out years ago. I've never been sure what it was about, but I don't think they've exchanged a word for at least five years!'

'Oh heck! Well, it was just an idea. Yes, I'll come with you. I just need to get changed out of my uniform and have my tea.'

'No problem. How about I call for you about six-ish?'

Louise's parents seemed surprised when she told them her plans for that evening. Her mother couldn't understand why she wanted to see Nora ever again, but her father always tried to see the good in everyone and thought it was a good idea.

'She'll be with Alfred anyway, Sandra, and he seems a sensible lad.'

So, she was allowed to go, and it turned out to be an interesting hour or so.

Nora opened the door a tiny amount, always suspicious, but broke into a big smile when she saw who it was.

'Alfred!' she exclaimed, giving him a big hug.

Louise was shocked, Nora was a different person at this moment. She looked so much kinder when she was smiling. She didn't think she'd seen her display that expression before, her face was usually creased up - frowning, criticizing, condemning.

And as Nora spotted her standing behind Alfie, the creases returned. Alfie, assessing the situation and trying to prevent bad feeling, pushed Louise in front of him. 'My new friend Louise wanted to meet you properly. She's only been in the Close a few months.'

Louise smiled at Nora, mentally thinking how quick Alfred was at dealing with the changing situation.

'Come in,' Nora said, politely but without the earlier enthusiasm she had displayed. They followed her through the narrow hallway, through the living room and into the dining room.

'Sit down,' she said, going into the kitchen to put the kettle on.

Alfred gave Louisa a reassuring wink.

'Do you both want tea?'

'Yes please.'

They told her how they liked it and Nora teased Alfred about his three sugars. 'You keep Silver Spoon in business single-handedly,' she laughed.

Louise had a look round the room. While the Thorpe's house had both rooms knocked into one, Nora's still had the separate rooms. This one had a dining table with four chairs and a big unit which took up one whole wall. On it were family photographs in frames, showing old black and white ones including what seemed to be Nora's wedding photo. Then more recent ones, teenagers in '80s fashions, which Louise guessed would be her grandchildren.

There were shelves of various chintzy ornaments and little trinkets and treasures which presumably meant something to Nora, but very little to anyone else. There were some books, including tens on sewing and a few drawers and closed cupboards which who-knew-what lie behind. Perhaps bones of her late husband? thought Louise.

She gave a start as Nora brought the drinks through, as though she'd been caught doing something naughty, but she composed herself quickly and they sat down around the table together, which was covered with a white tablecloth patterned with pretty pink and blue roses at the edges.

Alfred told her about the Christmas meal at the village hall, but she was quite dismissive and didn't seem keen. 'Hmm, I won't know anyone. I think I prefer my own company, thank you.'

He told her to think about it, but she quickly changed the subject. She quizzed Alfred about how long he was home and how his Navy life was going. She also asked about his love life.

'I saw that pretty girlfriend of yours, as I was looking out the window the other day.'

'What a surprise!' thought Louise. 'Fancy Nora looking out the window, spying on people. Who'd have thought it?' But she continued to smile and listen to the conversation, enjoying seeing another side to the woman that was still surprising to her. Mind you, everyone loved Alfie, she shouldn't be surprised that he brought out this warm, caring side to Nora.

He was telling Nora about Samantha. Louise drifted away from the conversation slightly, her eyes straying to the bookshelf again. Then she realised her name had been said and she hadn't heard it.

'Nora was asking how you were finding the school here,' Alfred repeated.

'Oh sorry, yes, it's good. The teachers are nice, and I have some good friends too. I was just noticing your sewing books, do you sew?'

'Yes, I do. Well, I used to. I haven't for a while now, though I still have my sewing kit. When my kids were younger, I'd sew most of their clothes. I really liked it.'

'Oh, I've just had my first couple of sewing lessons at school. I've been enjoying it. My mum doesn't really sew, she knits well though.'

'Maybe Nora could teach you,' interjected Alfred with a cheeky grin.

Louise shot him a look. She had been thinking of asking to borrow a book or two, not to see more of Nora!

Nora sighed. 'Maybe. It's been a while. I guess I haven't lost my touch, but who knows?' She took a drink of her tea. 'I'll have to get my bits out and see if I can still sew. My fingers aren't so nimble these days, what with the arthritis, but we'll see.'

She reached a large format hardback book off the shelf. 'Here. *Beginners' Guide to Sewing.* Have a look at that. Bring it back when you've finished with it. No hurry.'

'Thanks Nora, that looks great!'

She looked at Louise and gave her a smile, the first proper smile she had given her since she arrived on the doorstep.

Sandra was looking at the clock. 'They've been there a while!'

'Oh, stop worrying. Nora may be a pain, but she's not going to eat her or lock her in a cage like that witch in *Hansel and Gretel* or whatever. Besides, I trust Alfred, he'll look after her.'

'Do you think it's okay, her going there with him? I mean, he's much older than her.'

'Sandra! They're not dating, they're popping round a neighbour's house. Besides Alfred's engaged to Samantha.'

'But our Louise can be quite impressionable. She needs to be spending time with boys her own age.'

'She already does.'

'Really? Well, I've never seen her with any.'

'At the Bonfire Night, she was talking to a lad in her class. Toby. He seemed lovely. Quiet, a bit geeky maybe.'

'Well, she never mentioned him to me.'

'Perhaps she will do in time. You don't need to worry about her, she's only twelve. She'll discover boys in her own time. It's all gymnastics right now and that's not a bad thing!'

Honestly! His wife was never happy, she could always find something to worry about. He poured himself a small whisky, paused, then added a bit more. He felt he deserved it.

Only the next day in fact, Louise found herself hanging around with Toby at school. Jayne was off with a bad tummy - Louise suspected she had just started her period, as she herself had only a month ago. In the lunch hour, he asked if she wanted to go to the chess club with him. She was the only girl there, but all the boys welcomed her, and she stopped feeling shy after a few minutes.

She played a game with Toby, which she enjoyed. He beat her, but she didn't feel completely outclassed and Toby told her she had potential, she just needed to practice a bit more. As she couldn't remember the last time she'd played chess with her dad, she suspected he was right.

The next lesson after dinner was Drama and the class had to do activities in pairs. It seemed natural that Louise and Toby would pair up and the first thing that had to do was pretend to be their five-year-old selves and have a conversation with each other.

Louise started talking about playing with her dolls and her old house, how she had a red plastic phone in her Wendy house which she'd use to 'ring up' Batman, Robin and Commissioner Gordon to warn them of approaching dangers!

Toby's five-year-old self though had a much more tragic story. He spoke very quietly at first, saying how his little brother had been ill, then he had died. He was two years old, three years younger than Toby. He was visibly trying to control his emotions and Louise put her hand over his. He gave her as much of a smile as he could muster, appreciating the gesture.

'I'm sorry,' he said. 'I've not told anyone about it before.'

'That's okay, it's perfectly normal to be sad about something as awful as that.'

The second Drama task was much lighter and soon the classroom was full of strange animal sounds and giggles as they all had to move around the room pretending to be various creatures. But Toby's story stayed with her. In the afternoon break, she asked him if he'd like to come to her house for tea sometime. He seemed really thrilled to be asked and said he'd love to, so they agreed to talk to their parents and arrange something.

At the end of the school day, they walked part of the way home together. Toby lived in the middle of the village, whereas Louise's house was near the village hall, another five to ten minutes' walk.

'I'll see you tomorrow then, Toby.'

'Yes. And thanks, Louise. For what happened in Drama. You know, A lot of kids would have taken the Mick, but not you.'

'No, I'm not like that. Thank you for trusting me. See you tomorrow.'

'Bye.'

It seemed only a couple of minutes before she was home. She turned the key and skipped in through the front door. Her mum looked up from the book she was reading. 'You seem happy!'

'Yeah,' she said. 'I am.'

Sandra had arranged to go to Ruth and Brenda's house for coffee that morning. She was really struggling to get into the Charles Dickens they were supposed to be reading for book club. It just felt too much like being back at school again, when English Literature was a compulsory subject. It was sapping her love for reading, just as *Bleak House* had temporarily done when she studied it for A-level English Lit. She hoped her friends could find a way to ignite her interest in it – or perhaps just tell her what happens, so she didn't need to read it herself!

She took the dog for a quick walk first. She hadn't seen Martin since the book club but realised she'd been looking for him on her journeys around the village. People said villages were small, but how come when you wanted to find someone, you didn't?

She let Olga back in, then locked up. As she walked past Nora's house, she heard the front door opening. She put her head down and continued to walk, but a voice called her back.

'Erm, excuse me?'

She turned round. Nora was scurrying towards her. 'I'm sorry we got off on the wrong foot. Your girl popped round a couple of nights ago. I just wanted to say how lovely she is. A credit to you.'

'Thank you, that's very kind.'

They smiled awkward smiles, then Sandra ostentatiously checked her watch. 'Oops! Better go, I'm going to be late. See you later!'

Nora waved her off, then walked back into her house. Positioning herself on her favourite chair, with its perfect view of the street, she wrote in her little lined pad. 'Mrs. Thorpe, left street 9.58am.' She would be here, waiting, to see when she got back.

'Sorry I'm a bit late! Got waylaid by Nora.'

'Oh, it's not like we're the doctors or something. We don't tell you off!' laughed Ruth.

Brenda shouted through from the kitchen. 'What would you like to drink, Sandra?'

'Coffee please.'

She followed Ruth through into the lounge. These houses were a bit smaller than the ones in Whitlock Close, probably built around the same time, but two-bedroomed semis, not three. The women had decorated it all beautifully, with bright colours highlighting each room, tasteful statement walls or wall hangings and in the kitchen, the fitted cupboards were a pretty lemon colour, the kettle and toaster in bright red. It was arty and fun, and Sandra loved it. She knew she would never be able to persuade her conservative husband to do anything like this to their house, his tastes were definitely twenty years ago.

One of the cats jumped up beside her on the sofa. It was a friendly podgy tabby with bright green eyes. 'Hello Puss!', she said, rubbing under its chin. 'Which one's this?'

'Freddy, the other two are out. This one prefers to stay indoors most of the time. He's a real homebody. Likes his creature comforts.'

They chatted about pets and Dickens – Ruth had read the book but wasn't overly keen; Brenda had given up after it failed the Fifty Page Rule. ('If it hasn't grabbed you by fifty pages, it's not going to!') Sandra told them about the surprising change in Nora, then Ruth asked how Louise was getting on with her gymnastics.

'Oh, good thanks, she's loving the gym club. We got her a practice beam for her birthday, so she's outside on that whenever it's not too cold.'

'How old is she now?'

'Twelve.'

'Oh, a year younger than my Bryony,' commented Ruth. She stood up and reached a framed photo off the mantlepiece. Sandra held it, examining it. The photo was of a young girl playing on the beach, but she looked much younger than thirteen. As if Ruth knew what she was thinking, she said 'That was a few years ago. When I split up with her dad, Ken, she decided to live with him.'

'Are they local?'

'No, they moved down to Portsmouth, where Ken's from originally. His mother's elderly and quite disabled, so she needed permanent live-in help or to go into some kind of residential facility.'

'Do you see much of your daughter? She's very pretty. Looks like you.' (She wasn't sure that she did, but it was the sort of thing you said.)

Ruth smiled. 'No, not for a few years now. There was a bit of a scandal when I left Ken for Brenda. It wasn't really the done thing. We were living in Derbyshire then, a really tiny village, one of those where everyone knows everybody. Well, you can imagine! After Ken and Bryony moved down south, Brenda and I moved here.'

'Yes, we wanted a new start, where no-one knew our business.'

'The whispering and gossiping were getting tiresome. We don't need that kind of thing.'

'No-one does,' replied Sandra sympathetically. 'I always say you love who you love. I don't think you can choose who you love, it just happens. It may not be what society thinks it should be, but it is what it is. One of my friends in the city, she left her husband for a man twenty-five years older than her. They seem blissfully happy. Who's to judge?'

Ruth and Brenda smiled at her. 'We're so pleased you feel like that. It's great to have a friend who isn't judgmental.'

'Mind you,' reassured Brenda. 'This village isn't too bad; we don't get many voices shutting up as we walk in the pub or shop or whatever.'

'I think we're just seen as eccentrics!'

'Two old spinsters living together because they can't find husbands!' They all laughed.

'Mind you,' said Ruth, 'While they can ignore two women living together, that family moving into your street are going to rock the village, aren't they?'

'Into Whitlock Close?'

'Yes, the house that's been having all the work done. They wanted the attic converted into a proper bedroom, because they've got a few kids.'

'Oh, I did wonder what was happening there. Number nine, next to the Smallacres?'

'Yes, that's right.'

'So why will that rock the village?'

'They're black.'

Sure enough, a couple of days later, a big van arrived full of furniture and boxes and a large car full of people. Nora's curtains were constantly twitching, but when she couldn't see enough, she decided to go out and rearrange her bins and check how the plants in her front garden were getting on. Being November, they weren't doing much at all, but she still managed to spend a good twenty minutes checking how little they were doing.

After first of all noting the family were black, then counting how many children were getting out of the car, she had to go and sit down and make herself a strong cup of coffee. Things were changing in the village, and she wasn't always too happy about it.

After school, Louise and Jayne took Lady Olga out for a walk. When they got back into the Close, they saw two girls standing outside number nine. As they approached them, they saw Mitty was rubbing round their legs, which was the perfect introduction.

'Hi, I'm Louise, I live at number three. This is my dog Lady Olga and that's my cat Mitty.'

'Hi, I'm Jayne, I live up near the chippy.'

The girls smiled; they were both pretty with thick long black hair in braids. The taller one spoke first. 'Hi, I'm Faith and this is Grace. We've just moved in today. Your cat's lovely!'

'Are you going to New Barnham Secondary School?'

'Yes, we start on Monday, I'm fifteen, Grace is twelve.'

'Oh, we're twelve too, so we'll be in the same year as you.' Louise grinned at Grace, who had yet to say a word.

'Our dad's going to be the new GP here.'

'Oh lovely, where were you living before?'

'Birmingham, but it was getting a bit dangerous in places and our parents wanted us to grow up somewhere smaller and safer. They're from a small village in Nigeria originally and they found living in a big city rather intimidating.'

'Yes, I can understand that. I think this village is fairly quiet and safe.'

'Maybe not so quiet now you have a big family in the street!'

'I was the only child in the Close,' said Louise, 'so I'm thrilled to have you here.'

'Well, besides us two girls, we have two little brothers – Raymond is ten and Noah is six. We have an older brother too, but he has a job, so stayed in Birmingham with his girlfriend.'

'Wow! Five kids! I'd love a big family!'

'That's because you're an only child, Louise,' remarked Jayne. 'I've got a two-year-old brother called Harry and he's a nightmare! I'm never having kids when I'm older!'

They laughed, then Sandra popped her head out the front door.

'Louise, your tea's ready! Oh, hello girls, welcome to the village!'

'Thank you!' they replied.

'That's my mum, Sandra, my dad's Rob.'

'Our mum is called Beatrice, Dad's name is Chidi.'

'Oh, lovely names! Do you want to walk up to school with me on Monday? I walk on my own until we get to the village green, then meet up with Jayne to walk the rest of the way.'

'Yes, thanks, that would be perfect! Save us getting lost!'

'Brilliant. I'd better go in, before Mum gets mad! See you later!'

Louise went in for tea and Jayne walked home, knowing her mum would soon have her meal on the table too. Presuming she had been able to put Harry in his playpen for long enough to cook something… Grrr! Little brothers… Louise didn't know how lucky she was being an only child.

The conversation at the dinner table that evening was all about the new arrivals. Sandra was saying 'Ruth and Brenda reckon they're the first black family to move into the village.'

Louise nodded. 'Yes, there aren't any at school, only an Asian girl in the Fifth Year and a Chinese boy, I think he's in the Third Year. It's great though, I love having all kinds of friends. I'd love someone to move here from Romania or the USSR, that would be amazing!'

'Only if they liked gymnastics!' suggested her dad.

'Well yes, that would help, but even if they didn't, they could help me learn their language and how to say the names properly.'

She told her parents what the new family were called and how old the kids were.

'Five kids? Gosh, one's enough for me!'

'Thanks Mum!' Louise said sarcastically.

'I just couldn't have coped with anymore.'

'It's not like I'm a naughty child!' She was feeling a bit indignant now.

'No, I'm just not very maternal, I guess.'

Louise exchanged raised eyebrows with her father. Her mother often came out with things that veered from undiplomatic to downright tactless.

'I'm off up to my bedroom, I've got to write an essay for English.'

'Oh, okay, what's it about?'

'My favourite parent,' Louise joked.

When Louise left for school on Monday morning, Faith and Grace were already waiting for her outside.

'You can knock, you know,' she teased them.

They started walking up, out of the estate and up the alleyway past the village hall. Louise told them a few interesting bits as she walked past various parts of the village.

'Mum goes to the book club there. Are your parents big readers?'

'Mum is, yeah,' said Faith, 'and we all love books too, but Mum might like a book club.'

'You'll have to get her over to ours sometime, my mum can tell her all about it, to see if she would be interested.'

As they walked up towards the village green, they could see Jayne waiting for them, and Toby was with her. 'Hey, I found a waif and stray,' Jayne said to the girls. They introduced Toby to Faith and Grace and the five of them continued the walk to the secondary school, which was at the very end of the village with only fields and the road afterwards.

'Do you know which class you're both in?' asked Toby.

'No, we have to go to the reception desk, they told Mum. They'll sort everything out there.'

'Okay, I'll take you,' said Louise. 'I'll catch up with you two in a minute.' Jayne and Toby walked on.

The scary secretary, Mrs. George was there. She had her hair up in a tight grey bun that pulled her face upwards, though never into a smile. She always looked like she was on the verge of shouting. The kids called her 'The Dragon' for obvious reasons. Louise explained her neighbours were starting their first day at school. Mrs. George opened a big blue folder in front of her and asked 'Surname?'

'Achebe,' replied Faith.

Mrs. George looked over the top of her glasses. 'Spelt?'

'A-C-H-E-B-E.'

Finally finding the information she required, she said 'Oh yes, here we are. Faith, I'll get Miss. Green to take you to your class in a minute. Louise, Grace is in your class, are you okay to take her with you? Miss. Hill will sort everything out there.'

'Yes, of course, Mrs. George.'

As the secretary nipped into the office, Louise whispered to Faith 'It's okay, Miss. Green is the nice secretary, you'll be fine.'

Miss. Hill sat Grace next to Louise, next door but one to Jayne. Over the first two lessons and during break, and away from her big sister, Grace did start to come out of herself a bit more. They learnt that she was a good runner and had competed for her previous school at 100m and 200m, so she was interested to find out more about their P.E. and Games lessons. They all listened to the Top 40 every week on the radio and loved Blondie and Adam and the Ants.

Louise's dad always said you could find something in common with everyone and she thought that was true, you just had to work out what it was – and let's face it, most First Year girls would have lots in common. Although Grace was shy, Louise and Jayne already liked her. It was great for Louise to have more kids in Whitlock Close as well.

The Thorpe's cat Mitty often brought things home as presents for his humans. They were usually empty crisp packets and leaves he'd caught, which his humans praised him for, before depositing them surreptitiously in the bin. This evening though, he brought something rather different home.

'Mum! Dad!'

They came running at the urgency in their daughter's voice. She pointed and they looked outside the front door.

'Oh,' exclaimed Sandra. 'Mitty's found a friend. Better let them in then.'

'Yes,' agreed Robert. 'It looks starving, poor thing!'

Mitty's new friend was another cat, but it wasn't in great shape. Its fur was wiry and a bit matted and it looked very underweight. It followed Mitty into the house, looking left and right cautiously, seemingly very jumpy. When the front door closed, it ran behind the sofa but soon came out when a bowl of Whiskas was brought into the room.

The Thorpes retreated to the dining room, leaving the cat in peace.

'I wonder if it's got a home?'

'It doesn't look like it.'

'If it has got one,' piped up Louise angrily, 'they aren't looking after it properly.'

'We'll keep it here tonight, then I'll walk round the Close tomorrow to see if anyone knows who it belongs to.'

The next morning, after Louise had gone to school with the Achebe girls and Rob had gone off to work, Sandra began knocking on her neighbours' doors. She knew Sarah at number five had left for work too, so she'd check with her later, if need be. First of all, she went to see Old Mr. White at number one.

'Oh yes, that old tabby cat,' he answered her query. 'I shooed it off the other day. Always in 'ere, he is. Don't want them pets in my garden scaring me birds away.'

'Do you know who owns it?'

'Nope. Don't know where the cat comes from. I don't think anyone can own it because it's in such bad nick.'

She thanked him and went across the road to see Mabel at number fifteen. She opened the door with a big smile. 'Hello, you're the new lady from number three, aren't you? I've seen you at book club, but we haven't had a chance to chat really. How lovely to meet you properly, would you like a cup of tea?'

She said she would pop in for a cuppa another day but was trying to find out any information about the cat. Mabel also recognized it from her description, saying she had seen it hanging round for months and thought it was a stray.

By the time she had just set foot on Nora's drive, the Mini Menace was out there intercepting her. Once she explained to the elderly lady what her mission was, she backed up Old Mr. White and Mabel's accounts. 'Yes, old thing's been around for ages, always meowing for something.'

Sandra decided she'd gathered enough evidence and went inside to ring the village vets, who offered her an appointment that evening to check the cat over and see if they recognized it. Rob managed to finish work a bit early and they used Mitty's travel box to transport the tabby cat. The vet was a young woman, mid-twenties, chatty but efficient and she gave the cat a thorough check up.

'Definitely undernourished. Female, probably about seven to ten years old, I would think. Either a stray or neglected and no, we haven't seen her here before. I'm pretty sure I know all the pets in the village. Anyway, if anyone comes to claim her, ring the police because that's a serious case of neglect.'

They took the cat home with flea treatment, worm treatment and an assortment of things to put in her food to build her up. They also registered her with the vet.

When Louise later got home from gym club, she heard the news and said, 'So she's ours then?'

'I guess so.'

'And what have you called her?'

'It was your dad's idea.'

'Dad? What's her new name?'

'Tabby.'

'Tabby? Couldn't you think of anything original?'

'No. Sorry.'

'Well,' declared Louise. 'I'm going to call her Tabina. It sounds much nicer than Tabby!' She went upstairs to get bathed and changed out of her leotard and tracksuit. Sandra took the dirty clothes and put them in the washing machine with the rest of the laundry. She was already moaning about the amount of ironing she'd have to do the next day.

Rob poured himself a whisky and settled down to watch *Hi-de-Hi!* on BBC One. Lady Olga jumped up onto his lap, Mitty sat one side of him and Tabby – not quite daring to jump up on the sofa yet – snuggled down by his feet.

It was the last week of term and only a week until Christmas, so all the kids were madly excited. The teachers had given up teaching them proper schoolwork and instead were concentrating on fun activities. Some kids had brought in mistletoe from the Christmas market and the teachers were trying to curb the kissing a bit, without stamping all over their fun! It was often a hard balance to get right.

Louise, Jayne and Cally had taken part in the end-of-year gymnastics display and that afternoon, the choir were going to be performing and a group of dancers from the Fifth Year. The children were all very excitable in the dinner break, running around even more than usual and shouting at an even higher level.

Louise, Jayne, Toby and Grace were chatting together, laughing over something one of their teachers had said earlier, when three girls walked over towards them. It was Natalie, Suki and Tara from the Second Year, and they never came over for any good reason, they were troublemakers and usually looking for a fight.

'So, New Girl,' Suki said to Grace. 'Where you from then?'

'Whitlock Close, I live near Louise,' she answered politely.

Natalie laughed in her face. 'Nah. Originally?'

'I'm from Birmingham.'

The three girls laughed again. 'No, you're not British, your skin isn't the right colour.'

'I am British, I was born in Birmingham.'

'Bet you don't even celebrate Christmas!' sneered Tara.

Grace had been slowly moving backwards during this conversation and was now pressed up against the wall. She could retreat no further.

Suddenly Toby moved between the three girls and Grace. 'Leave her alone! She's as much right to be here as any of us. She hasn't done anything wrong!'

The girls were shocked. The mousey looking nerdy boy had spoken out! Natalie moved up close to him. 'And what business is it of yours, smart arse?'

'What you're doing is being racist,' he replied, fluffing up his chest and standing tall. 'It's a crime!'

'So what?' they challenged him.

'My dad's a policeman, I'll report you to him.'

Tara went right up to his face, looking like she was about to spit at him, but Natalie pulled her back. 'Come on, leave these stupid idiots alone, they're welcome to their *coloured* friend!'

As they walked away, Louise sighed with relief. 'Well done, Toby, you were fab!'

'Yes thanks,' said Grace, wiping away a tear. Jayne gave her a quick hug.

'I didn't know your dad was a policeman?'

'Oh, he's not,' grinned Toby. 'He's a milkman. But they weren't to know that.'

The bell rang and they headed off towards their classroom. Louise squeezed Toby's hand and, when no-one was looking, gave him a quick kiss on the cheek. 'You're a hero!' she told him. He was still blushing when they walked in.

Christmas 1981

Louise loved Christmas; it was her favourite time of year. Her family were big fans too and they socialized at one another's houses across several days, so it was a long and happy celebration. For as long as she could remember, they had all gone to eat Christmas dinner at a hotel nearby. Presents in the morning, hotel dinner, then a walk in the grounds before going home.

Boxing Day would usually be at one aunt and uncle's house, another day's party at the other aunt and uncle's, then half a day at her Gran's house. Her Nanna's birthday was in early January, so that was another half a day and she loved it all. She really enjoyed spending time with everyone.

One aunt and uncle hadn't any children, but Louise still enjoyed their company and they always had a great collection of board games to play. Her other aunt and uncle had three children – Samuel was a couple of months older than her, then Laura was sixteen and Rachael nineteen. Louise looked up to her older female cousins and they would give her their old magazines and annuals which she loved reading, things like *Blue Jeans* and *Jackie*. She would ask them about make-up and fashion, it was like having big sisters.

Plus, there were the presents, of course! One advantage to being an only child of a middle-class family was that she usually got the main present she wanted. She wasn't spoilt, she could still remember things she had wanted but hadn't got (Weebles, Shaker Maker and the Game of Life!) but she always loved the gifts they got her. She still played with her *Doctor Who* doll and her *Charlie's Angels* dolls. (Cheryl Ladd was her favourite!) This year, she received books (a staple gift!), clothes, a new leotard, a new

Sindy doll, some gymnastics books and a Rubik's cube, which was the latest thing. Toby could complete the whole thing in a few minutes, but she was stuck at two sides!

One year, when she'd been maybe eight, she had sneaked into her parents' bedroom and found most of her presents hidden there, unwrapped. That Christmas had been the most disappointing one ever. She'd had no surprises but still had to pretend everything was unexpected. She learnt her lesson and never did that again.

A week or so before New Year, the Thorpes decided they should throw a New Year's Eve party. They only invited those in the Close, plus Ruth and Brenda, and Louise invited Jayne and Toby. It was the first time they'd had a big 'do' in their new house. Sandra loved the panicking and complaining involved in planning a party. She would worry about the catering and if they had enough drinks in, then a couple of days before, she'd be perusing her double fitted wardrobe stuffed with clothes and caterwauling how she had "nothing to wear." Louise and Rob were well used to her by now, of course, so their reactions veered from false sympathy to mumbled 'Yes, dear's from Rob to both of them finding something urgent to do in a different part of the house. 'She loves it really!' whispered Louise to her dad after one particularly heartfelt session of whining.

They took the handwritten invitations round the Close and everyone was pleased to get one, though Old Mr. White said he probably wouldn't come over, as he wasn't a fan of New Year's and tended to be in bed early. Rob assured him they wouldn't play music too loud, but Old Mr. White touched his arm, saying 'It's fine, I'm quite deaf once I take these hearing aids out at night, you do what you want, lad!'

Mabel and Nora were both unsure whether they would come but thanked them for their kindness.

'Why on earth aren't those two good friends?' Rob commented to his daughter. 'They could really be a support to one another.'

'I agree, Dad, but Alfie said they had some big falling out years ago and they're both too stubborn to get over it. They haven't said a word to each other in years.'

Rob shook his head. 'Well, it seems silly to me. Perhaps we can do a bit of meddling and sort them out?' He didn't like conflict.

The Smallacres and the Achebe family were very excited about the party and said they'd all come over, thanks for asking us. Hugh said he couldn't come for the whole evening, but he would certainly pop over for a drink. Sarah Willington said she'd love to drop in at some point, but that her boyfriend Mark was staying over. Rob said of course, bring him too, that's fine, the more the merrier and they would look forward to meeting him.

Despite all the panicking and complaining, everything was ready by eight in the evening and Sandra had managed to "throw something on" that she deemed adequate for the event. Louise and Jayne had decided to both wear their ra-ra skirts and Robert had grabbed something straight out of the wardrobe that would probably do.

Toby arrived at quarter past eight, dropped off by his dad, who said he'd pick him up just gone midnight. The Smallacres turned up next – Chloe, Gerry, Alfie and the glamorous Samantha (Glam Sam as Louise nicknamed her) and the Achebes were a few minutes behind, a splash of happy noise and brightly coloured clothes. Ruth and Brenda turned up with a bottle of wine and a homemade carrot cake, which they added to the table.

Louise and Jayne had been warned to avoid drinking any alcohol until midnight, when they were allowed a small flute of champagne each. Jayne was staying over, and Mrs. Thorpe was adamant she was not going to cover for a second hangover! The chastised twelve-year-olds were sipping Coca-Cola when Faith and Grace walked over to them. Raymond had headed straight for the bowls of crisps on the table and Noah was shyly staying close to his mum. Lady Olga suddenly appeared and sat cutely, looking at Raymond with her big brown eyes, hoping for a crisp or ten.

When Toby arrived, Faith introduced him to her parents who thanked him for standing up to the bullies at school, on behalf of their daughter. Mr. Achebe insisted he take a five pound note for their gratitude and Toby said it was nothing, any of them would do the same thing, but he accepted the money gratefully. He walked over to the girls, bright red to the edges of his ears.

'Our hero!' said Faith, nudging him.

'Aww stop it! Toby doesn't like being the centre of attention, do you?' commented Louise.

'No, I don't, I much prefer to fade into the background!'

'Talking of which,' added Jayne. 'Who the hell is that hunk that Sarah's just brought in?'

They all turned to look and yes, he was certainly hunky – over six feet tall, short dark hair and one of those dazzling smiles usually only sported by American film stars.

'Wow, she's done alright for herself!' Faith said, letting out a low wolf whistle.

'Shh, he'll hear you!' giggled Jayne.

Sarah was just introducing her boyfriend to Sandra and Rob, so Louise nipped over to find out more, turning up just in time to hear the lowdown. Her girl friends looked on jealously as the man shook hands with Louise and Rob and kissed Sandra on the cheek. They couldn't wait for her to return and tell them all she'd found out.

'Well?' they asked her.

'He's a pop star!'

'What?'

'He's called Mark and he's a guitarist in The Unflappables.'

'I haven't heard of them.'

'Me neither.' They all shook their heads.

'They've had a number three hit in America. They've been over there most of the time but are here now and planning to crack the UK.'

'How exciting!'

'So how did Sarah meet him?' asked Jayne.

'Mum asked the same thing. Apparently, Sarah's older brother is a music producer or something in London, she was up there a few months ago and her brother introduced her to Mark, and they hit it off straightaway!'

'Well, you would, wouldn't you?' Faith was still watching him from a distance. 'He's lovely!'

'Ooh look out,' said Jayne, 'Glam Sam's making a beeline for the best-looking guy in the room!'

And she was! In her tight fitting red mini dress, she sauntered over to him. 'Hi, you're Mark Thomas from The Unflappables, aren't you? I saw you on TV all the time when I was in New York,' they heard her say.

'Bloody hell!' Louise sneered. 'How's that for a chat up line?'

Both Alfie and Sarah had overheard the exchange, as Mark politely asked Samantha about her connections to New York. Alfie had just filled a plate up and headed over to where his girlfriend was drooling at another man. 'Here you go, Darling,' he said to her, nodding at Mark pleasantly and handing Sam the food. 'I thought you might fancy a sausage,' holding one up on a cocktail stick. She took the plate ungraciously and walked off towards the drinks table.

Alfie grinned at Mark. 'Sorry mate.'

'It's fine. Don't worry, some of them get a little starstruck.'

Alfie followed Sam over to the drinks and grabbed a can of beer from the ice bucket.

'How dare you!' His girlfriend was livid. 'I was talking to Mark. He's an important person, he'd be good for my career.'

'You were embarrassing yourself, Sam!'

She poured herself a glass of wine and stalked out into the garden, sitting by herself on a chair near the pond. She wished she smoked, then she could really piss off Alfie, who was very anti anything unhealthy.

Suddenly she heard a cough from the side of her. Hugh emerged out of the dark corner of the garden.

'Ah, another loner,' he smiled at her. 'I'm much happier by myself too.' He was slurring a bit and Sam noticed he had a couple of bottles on the ground nearby. 'I popped in via the back gate and have been trying to get up the confidence to come in and say hi. Maybe I'll manage it after this bottle's finished.' He started to laugh but ended up having a coughing fit instead.

'Oh, are you okay?'

He nodded. 'I'll be fine. I just have a few health problems. Don't worry about it.'

He pulled up a chair and sat beside her. She sipped her wine.

'I live at number eleven. I was at your Alfie's Welcome Home party, but I don't think we spoke there.'

'No, I don't remember you.'

'I didn't stay long. I struggle a bit with social functions.'

She looked at him closer. 'What's your name?'

'Hugh.'

'Hugh what?'

He laughed. 'Stephenson.'

'*The* Hugh Stephenson? Of *Small Satires* fame?'

'Yes, 'fraid so. In another time, another life. Did you watch it then?'

'Oh yes, it was really popular, wasn't it? Brilliantly clever, my mum loved it.'

'Oh thanks. Yes, it was a bit alternative. Fell out of fashion.'

'It was ahead of its time; you lot were great!'

'Thank you. That's very kind of you to say.'

Sam heard her name being called. She turned round to see Alfie.

'I'm off home, Sam, Mum's not feeling too well. She's had too many wines. Are you coming or staying?'

'I'll come. See you later, Hugh, take care.'

Hugh finished the second bottle, then went home via the back gate. He'd not found the courage to go into the house and mingle after two bottles and was loathe to try a third. Anyway, the dogs would be missing him.

Samantha couldn't believe she had met two famous people in one night! Wow! She was desperate to tell Alfie about who Hugh was, but she'd wait for Chloe to stop throwing up first.

Gerry stayed at the party. He had been drinking slower than his wife and sitting chatting happily to Rob, as usual. In fact, they were just discussing the possibility of sneaking away somewhere wife-free for a weekend of cricket watching. They decided that would be something safe to suggest, as neither wife would have any interest in it.

'And we could always find a decent pub near the cricket ground!'

They clicked their glasses together.

'To the plan!'

'The plan!'

None of the elderly residents had turned up to the party. Mabel's curtains were all drawn, so she had presumably gone to bed, but Nora's were open, and they could see she had a light on.

'She's probably just watching us,' mused Louise to her mother.

'It's sad really.' Sandra was seeing Nora differently since Louise had visited and told her a few more details about Nora's family and her lonely solitary life.

'If Alfie was still here, he could have gone over and tried to persuade her to come across.'

'Yeah, sadly he had to get Chloe back before she was sick.'

They looked over at the Smallacres house.

'I wonder why Hugh didn't come over.'

As it approached midnight, Rob turned on the TV so they could all watch the fireworks from London and the countdown to the New Year.

10, 9, 8, 7, 6, 5, 4, 3, 2, 1….

January 1982

'Happy New Year!' everyone shouted. They sang *Auld Lang Syne* and toasted each other with their glasses of champagne, going round hugging and kissing people they loved, liked and some they didn't know. Mark received a surprising number of kisses from women he hardly knew, but he didn't seem to mind too much.

'Wow! 1982! We'll be teenagers this year!' Louise said to her school friends. 'How weird is that?'

'I won't,' moaned Jayne.

'Oh I forgot you're not twelve till July. Sorry!'

'I'll be sixteen!' Faith reminded them.

'Old enough to get married!' they teased her.

'I'd have to find a boyfriend first!'

'There must be someone you fancy, Faith! Your Year is full of handsome boys.'

'Oh, they may be handsome, Jayne, but if they are, they're not my type.'

'Do you know what your type is then? Because I don't know mine,' moaned Jayne.

'Nah, not really,' replied the older girl. 'I think once I meet him, I'll know. I'll realise he's different special somehow…'

Toby and Louise caught each other's eye and smiled. They both understood exactly what Faith meant.

A few minutes later, Beatrice Achebe came over to fetch the girls. 'Come on, you two, home time, your little brother's already asleep.'

They looked over at their father and saw he had Noah in his arms, the little boy's eyes tightly shut. Raymond was still standing, but yawning and rubbing his eyes.

They said their goodbyes, quickly followed by Sarah and Mark then Ruth and Brenda. Sandra saw the headlights of a car pass slowly by their window. 'Toby! I think this is your dad.'

'Thanks, Mrs. Thorpe!' he said. Louise walked him to the hall and passed him his coat.

'It's been lovely to see the New Year in with you,' he said.

'Me too.'

She looked behind her. The door was almost closed behind them, no one could see them. She leant forward and kissed him. He kissed her back. It was only for a couple of seconds, but it was the nearest thing to a snog that either of them had ever had.

They were looking at each other, as his dad knocked on the door. 'Will you be my girlfriend?'

She nodded. 'Yes. I'd love that!'

He grinned and winked at her, then opened the door and got into the car and went home.

Louise just stood there for a minute. It was January. It was 1982 and she had her first boyfriend. It was going to be a good year.

Jayne and Gerry were the last guests remaining. They both offered to help clear up. Jayne was staying the night anyway and Sandra suspected Gerry was avoiding going home to his drunk wife! Either way, all help was welcome, and they soon tidied up, filling up bin bags with bits of rubbish, used serviettes, half-eaten plates of food and abandoned cocktail sticks. They packed the food that was left into Tupperware containers, so it didn't go to waste. Gerry was told to help himself to anything he wanted and took home a container of nibbles he thought they would eat the next day.

As they waved goodbye to him, Rob went off to make himself and Sandra a cuppa and to feed the pets, who had taken themselves off when the house became crowded. Louise and Jayne declined the offer of a drink and went upstairs to get ready for bed.

'What is it?' asked Jayne. 'You've got a grin a mile wide. What happened?'

Louise pushed her into the bedroom and shut the door behind them. She was breathless with running up the stairs and trying to hide her excitement from her parents.

'Toby asked me to be his girlfriend! And I said yes!'

'Yippee!' squealed Jayne, giving her best mate a hug. 'That's fab!'

'And – we had a kiss!'

'Ooh, tell me everything!'

It was January 4th and thirty-six-year-old Robert Thorpe was as excitable as a child! Louise less so, but slightly, while Sandra had planned an extra ironing session.

'But aren't you going to watch, Sandra?' asked her husband.

'It's *Doctor Who*! A kids' programme!'

They regularly had this discussion. It always went the same way.

'No, it's not, it's a family show. For all ages.'

'I bet it won't be as good now,' contributed Louise. 'Not since Tom Baker isn't the Doctor anymore.'

'Oh yes,' recalled her mother. 'It's that vet bloke, isn't it?'

'Peter Davison. Yes.'

'He's a bit young to be Doctor Who, isn't he?'

'I thought you weren't interested,' mumbled Rob, close to defiance. He had watched *Doctor Who* since its first episode in 1963 and wasn't about to miss one now.

A few days later, the new school term began and the kids soon settled back into their old routine. Louise, Jayne, Grace and Toby were definitely a little gang now and Grace was becoming less shy as she got to know them all better. This term, the school were doing Cross Country running, the bane of many a secondary school pupil's life! However, Grace discovered she enjoyed it. At her previous school, she had been a sprinter, but with her new school being at the edge of a village, the course was interesting, going through fields and trees, even over a stream at one point. Grace felt free, she had hated the greyness of Birmingham and relished the outdoors and being close to nature like they were in New Barnham.

Over the weeks, Grace regularly won her races and soon the P.E. teacher was asking if she fancied representing the school at the

Inter-School Cross Country Championships coming up in March. She was thrilled! Mrs. Leighton explained she would need to put in some extra training, but she was happy to do that.

Louise and Toby were very discreet about their relationship at school. They had no desire to become a target of gossip or have their names scrawled across toilet walls. They were together a lot, but never kissed or held hands at school unless they were completely sure that no one could see them. Of course, some kids asked them outright if they were boyfriend and girlfriend, but they just said they were good friends – and they were. It was only their closest friends that knew the truth and they could be relied on to keep schtum.

Outside school though, they spent a lot of time together, often with other friends but sometimes just the two of them. They would take Lady Olga for a walk, or go to the shops together, or just sit on swings in the park and chat. They also went to each other's houses for tea and watched television, listened to records or played games of chess. Louise was improving, but she still couldn't beat him.

Theirs was a gentle romance, they were content to hold hands when they could, with their little kisses still in single figures. They had no wish to be like Sabrina and Paul. Rumours were already going round the school that those two had gone all the way – whatever that meant exactly.

Their parents were still unaware of their relationship, though they had talked about telling them soon.

Life for Sandra Thorpe was back to the old routine of housework, looking after the pets and trying to fit in her needs after those of her husband, her daughter, the dog and now two cats! She occasionally had a coffee with Chloe (though still found her annoying, so didn't want to make it too regular a thing!) and had started meeting up with Beatrice every couple of weeks. She was a lovely lady and they got on really well. She was the opposite of Chloe in many ways, Beatrice had no desire to gossip or pry, she was happy to be told whatever they wanted to tell her and no more. She would offer support or advice if asked, but never butted in when it was unwanted.

She had agreed to go to book club with Sandra but couldn't make it this week as Raymond was doing some after-school thing the same day. Brenda and Ruth were away too, Brenda's sister was getting married, and they'd gone down to Cardiff for the week. So, Sandra guessed that book club would be quite sparse this time.

As she walked in though, there were at least eight or ten people already there. One of them was Martin and he waved to her, indicating the empty chair next to him, which she sat in gratefully.

'Hi, how are you?' she asked him. 'I haven't seen you walking the dog.'

'No, Scamp's been ill, we've been at the vets quite a lot.'

'Oh, is he okay now?'

'Yes, he should be, he had to have an operation on his paw, but he'll be back walking in a few days.'

'Oh, we'll have to take him and Lady Olga out together. She could do with socializing with a few dogs.'

She was kicking herself inside. That was a stupid thing to say, and she didn't know why those words had come out of her mouth. Luckily Martin smiled and agreed it would be a good idea.

Belinda brought the meeting to attention and began proceedings.

'We've finished with Dickens, haven't we? I gave up on *Underwhelming Expectations*!' she whispered to Martin. He tried to contain his laughter, so as not to offend Belinda, who liked people to take the book club quite seriously!

While Belinda was talking, Sandra looked around the room. She recognized them all now – Beryl, Henry, Pauline, Mabel from her Close, Stanley, Debra (another woman around her age who hadn't been going long), plus a few she couldn't yet name – oh and Hugh was here too. He was sat in the far corner, listening intently, head down and eyes half-closed, so she couldn't catch his eye to wave.

As this was a kind of catch-up meeting, they were discussing which books they had been reading since the last meeting. Sandra hadn't read anything, she'd been too busy with Christmas, New Year and back to school preparations, so her contribution was minimal. Martin had read a lot though, mainly while waiting for the vets to ring him with news or sitting on the sofa cuddling a sad Scamp. His favourite read had been *Gorky Park* by Martin Cruz Smith, which had been released the previous year. He seemed to read a variety of genres though and said he enjoyed keeping up with the latest books and discovering new authors.

'Wow, he just gets better and better!' she found herself thinking, then immediately chastised herself. She was a happily married woman, a mum, she didn't need to be thinking stupid thoughts about another man. But she had to admit she found Martin fascinating. And was she happily married, when she looked at it? These days, her and Rob hardly seemed to do anything together. He went to various events for work, but she tended to stay at home, apart from the book club. She used Louise as an excuse, saying she didn't want to leave her by herself, but she was twelve, so could be left alone for a few hours. There were also plenty of potential babysitters in the Close who'd be happy to have her for an evening. Maybe she should see if something good was coming to the theatre or the cinema and see if she could arrange a night out, just her and Rob?

Even after these thoughts, when Martin asked her if she fancied walking the dogs together at half nine on Monday morning, she found herself saying yes without even pretending to consider her answer first.

At the end of the meeting, she tried to find Hugh, but he'd left, he must have gone while she'd nipped to the loo. She said goodbye to Martin and walked home with Mabel, discussing their next book they would be reading this month – *The Great Gatsby* by F. Scott Fitzgerald. Sandra hadn't read much American literature apart from a brief flirtation with John Steinbeck. She'd adored *Of Mice and Men*, but *The Grapes of Wrath* had brought that brief love affair to a close, moving Steinbeck into her list of Authors to Avoid along with Charles Dickens. And Barbara Cartland. At least Dickens had avoided the pink rinse.

As arranged, Martin came over to Sandra's at the appointed time on Monday with his dog. She already had Lady Olga on the lead, who was excited to go out, exchanging interested sniffs with Scamp.

'I thought we could just walk round the estate, if that's okay? Olga seems to have a bit of a sore paw today, so I don't want to take her too far.'

'No, that's fine, I've got to go to the Post Office later anyway. Pay some bills. All the boring stuff.'

They had a small Post Office in one corner of the Co-op. It was a godsend for those who didn't drive but needed to collect their pensions or benefits or had something to post.

They walked happily in silence for a while, Sandra pointing out little things of interest like where Ruth and Brenda lived, and which dogs would be looking out their windows. Then she told him about Christmas and what Louise had been given.

'I wish we had been able to have kids, you know. My wife and I.'

'Oh, I'm sorry. Was there some kind of, er, problem?'

'We never found out. It caused us all sorts of issues though. She tried some treatment. Hormonal. But it made her so temperamental, she was a hard woman to live with.'

'That must have been difficult for both of you.'

'I'm so glad she's out of my life.' He sounded really angry, as though this was a new pain he wasn't yet dealing with.

'Did you resent having to move out of your old home?'

'I did, I hated her for it! She ruined everything!'

She wasn't sure what to say. This was so different to his normal demeanour. She decided it was safer to change the subject.

'How does Scamp get along with cats? Lady Olga is fine with Mitty, they took to each other straightaway, and she has accepted

Tabby now too. She doesn't seem bothered about cats at all, she doesn't ever growl at them or chase them.'

'No, Scamp doesn't. He occasionally looks at them as though they might be part of a fun game. But he gives up before he actually bothers to do any chasing!' He was laughing along now, as though he hadn't said the previous few sentences. Sandra noted it was a delicate subject and not to mention his wife or his former life at any time in the future.

They walked round the estate without further incident, until they reached the top of Whitlock Close. 'Right, I'd better get in then, Martin, check this one's paw again.'

'No problem, Sandra, enjoyed the walk!'

'See you at the book club!'

'Bye!'

Nora watched her walk back into the Close, wave at some man she didn't recognize then go into her house with the little spaniel. She opened her little lined pad. 'Mrs. Thorpe arrived back in street 10.22am. With dog.'

February 1982

It was already February! Sandra still hadn't been for that cuppa with Mabel and seeing the old woman putting out her bins reminded her she should. It must be a lonely life living on your own without family nearby. As soon as she'd finished her morning chores, she popped across to number fifteen. Mabel was thrilled to see her, making her feel even more guilty that she'd left it so long.

'How are you?' Mabel asked, fussing with the kettle in the kitchen. 'And how's the tabby cat settling in?'

'Oh yes, really well, thanks. She's still a bit shy, but they're quite a family now, the dog and cats.'

'Ah I do miss having pets.'

'Why don't you get one, Mabel?'

'Well I couldn't walk a dog. I mean, I can do the odd trip to the book club or the Co-op, but I couldn't commit to dog walking every day. Sometimes I'm struggling to get round the house.'

'Thanks,' she said, accepting the cup of tea in the best China cups. 'A cat then?'

'That would certainly be easier. I'll think about it!'

They sat on either end of the three-seater sofa, its faded flowers fitting in with the rest of the décor – smart once, but had seen better days. Sandra wondered if she had any family and looked round the room as she sipped her tea. Noticing a black and white photo of a wedding day, she asked Mabel 'Oh is that you? What a beautiful photo!'

'Oh yes!' She got up and brought the framed picture over so Sandra could see it close up. 'That's me and Derek. We got married in 1945, after the War. When he got back safely, we decided it was time to tie the knot. We'd been apart so much. I was thirty-seven there, he was forty. I was old for a bride back then. Thought I'd never make it up the aisle!' She laughed.

'True love, eh? You look very happy!'

'Oh we were, we really were. Thing is, by the time we got married, then bought a house, we never seemed to have time to try for a family. That's the one thing I regret really. You're so lucky to have your Louise. She seems a lovely girl.'

Sandra smiled. Mabel was in full flow, and she wanted her to continue. She was enjoying hearing about her neighbour's life, and it was obvious Mabel was enjoying talking to someone.

'We'd not long moved in here when Derek died. 1975. He was seventy. Lung cancer. It was a shock though. Took him very sudden.'

'And you've never thought of looking for someone else? That's a long time to be on your own. You must get lonely.'

She sighed. 'Well I do, that's true. I've got the book club of course and I pop up to the shops or the library, find someone to have a natter with there. But no, I've never found another man friend, not since Derek. I'm not sure it would be right. We were soulmates.'

'Obviously no one could replace him, Mabel, but you might find yourself a friend, a good man to spend some time with sometimes.'

'I think I'm more likely to get a cat!' She smiled and Sandra returned the expression warmly, vowing to see more of Mabel, maybe talk to Beatrice and Chloe to see if they could visit her too. She didn't like thinking of people being lonely. She was aware her own mother had been widowed a decade now, but at least she had her dancing friends as well as family not far away.

It was Sandra's thirty-seventh birthday on February 8th so the day before, as it was a Sunday, the three of them went out for a meal. They went back into Lincoln to a family pub they used to eat in quite often when they lived nearby. It was a warm, homely kind of pub that cooked decent food like homemade steak pie and chips and where the staff knew the names of all the regulars. They had a lovely meal, but Sandra was feeling slightly depressed about heading towards her forties. Sometimes she felt so old, unattractive and unnoticed. As Louise was getting older, she needed her less and less too, so that Sandra was wondering what her role in life was. Maybe she should look into getting a part-time job?

For the Thorpe family overall though, February was all about Louise's gymnastics competition against Nottingham Gym Club. Louise's parents, Cally's parents and Jayne's dad were all going to Nottingham to cheer on the girls. Jayne's mum had decided to stay at home with little Harry, who was very likely to shout out in the middle of someone's beam routine.

They had been practicing hard for so long and knew all their routines really well. Louise was always talking about 'repetitions' and 'muscle memory' and her parents knew every note of her floor music by heart, so much that it haunted their dreams and they would wake up with it playing in their ears. They hoped she would change it after this competition!

The City Gymnastics Club team all travelled on a minibus looking very smart and professional wearing their green club leotards and matching tracksuits. They knew Nottingham were a stronger side, they had better facilities and already had a couple of their girls in the Great Britain national training squad. But everyone was determined to enjoy themselves, do their best and try to show their highest quality routines.

The teams consisted of eight girls per club, split into two sessions of four girls. Half the City team began on vault, competing against half the Nottingham team, then the other teams of four competed together on the bars. Louise and Jayne were relieved to start on the vault, as bars was still their weakest event. Both performed competent handsprings for decent scores, but the top Nottingham girls were doing half on – half off vaults and handsprings with full twists, which were much more complex and usually scored higher. Apparently one girl could do a Tsukahara but wasn't risking it today due to an ankle injury. Over on bars, Cally hit her routine, but only scored a 6.30.

Louise and Jayne knew their bars routines were low on difficulty and although performed well, their scores were 5.50 and 5.75. All the Nottingham girls were scoring in the 7.00s and 8.00s. 'I bet they went on bars as toddlers!' commented Louise to Jayne. Meanwhile, there were several falls on beam, but one of the top girls from Nottingham scored a 9.00! Cally stayed on the beam and included a back flip, which increased her difficulty and she got 7.85, which she was thrilled about. The girls all gave her hugs when she came over to them.

Jayne had a wobbly time on the beam, but managed not to fall off, knowing that a fall meant you lost 0.5 of a mark. Louise managed to conquer her nerves well, hit all her moves and stuck her barani dismount for a 7.30, so she was thrilled. Meanwhile in the other group, Cally introduced her new back layout somersault on the floor for 8.25.

Louise and Jayne finished their competition on floor. This was Louise's favourite apparatus and the audience responded to her cute dance movements and catchy music. Her tucked front and back somersaults weren't as hard as others did though and her score was 7.65. Jayne's routine was at a similar level, but her dance was a bit more contained, and she received 7.30. Cally finished on vault with a 7.00.

The Nottingham team beat them by twenty points! One of their girls performed a double twist on floor and three others did full twists, so that pulled their scores up into the 8.00s and a top mark of 9.40. The City girls were definitely outclassed. Out of the sixteen girls competing, the Nottingham girls easily took all the individual medals. Cally finished 7th, Louise 10th and Jayne 12th.

They were a bit disheartened in the minibus on the way home, but the girls had earned their first medals, as they all received a silver medal for the team coming second. Admittedly, there were only two teams, but Louise still hung it up over her bedroom mirror and every time she looked at it, it made her smile. Maybe she'd win a gold medal sometime? That was her dream.

Dr. Chidi Achebe was not having a good day at work. He'd had three people refuse to see him. One old woman came into the room, looked at him in horror and walked back out into the reception, saying she wasn't going to have any "black hands on her varicose veins!" He had forgotten the downsides to living in a small village. Birmingham was so multi-cultural that they hadn't really experienced any racism, yet they'd been in New Barnham for just two months and both him and his daughters had faced verbal attacks. Maybe he'd been wrong moving here? Yet he saw how rough some parts of Birmingham were becoming and he didn't want his kids to be living in an area where there were drugs and knife crime. He wanted to keep them all safe and thought this village would be the answer.

There was a knock at the door and Dr. Millhouse, who owned the practice, came in and sat down.

'I'm so sorry, Chidi, I can't apologise enough. We are going to have to rethink this, maybe find a way of introducing you to the village, so some of them can get over this stupid discrimination. In the meantime, take a couple of weeks off. Paid leave, of course.'

'My job's not in danger, is it?'

'No! No way! Don't you worry about that. You're not at fault here, you aren't the problem. Go home and I'll be in touch.'

The next morning, Sandra went over to Beatrice's for a coffee. She was surprised to find Chidi there, sat on the sofa in casual clothes, and she was even more surprised to hear what had happened.

'That's just appalling! It wasn't anyone we know, was it?' she asked him, wondering if Nora was racist. She wouldn't put it past her.

'No one I know and nobody from the Close. Such a shame though.'

'Definitely!'

'Not to blow my own trumpet, but I'm highly qualified, I've worked in Africa and in the UK and I can bring lots of knowledge and expertise to help people. It's so frustrating when they can't see past my skin colour.'

As she was leaving the Achebe's house, Chloe rapped on the window to get Sandra's attention then came to the front door. 'Come in for a coffee!' she shouted. Sandra agreed, although she'd had two at Beatrice's and would be needing the loo soon. But it seemed Chloe had important news to impart, so she followed her into the lounge and sat down, while the kettle boiled.

'It's quiet today,' Sandra remarked, noting the three Chihuahuas were outside, their evil little faces staring through the big glass window of the back door. She was sure one of them was baring its teeth at her in a threatening way. It reminded her of the film she'd seen last August – *An American Werewolf in London*.

'Yes, everyone's out,' replied Chloe, coming in holding two colour-coordinated mugs. She saw Sandra looking at the dogs. 'They've got such cute faces, haven't they?' Sandra murmured something indecipherable through a sip of the hot drink. Well, she could hardly bring up the werewolf, could she? Luckily Chloe failed to notice the lack of response.

'Alfred's dumped Samantha.'

'What?'

'Yes. Well, you know what she was like at your New Year's Eve party?'

Sandra thought 'I know what *you* were like too. I'm locking up the booze next time you come over!' but just verbalized one word - 'Yes.' She knew Chloe would happily continue with the story, whether questions were asked or not, or indeed whether any interest was shown. But Sandra was interested. She hadn't liked Sam and thought Alfie could do a lot better for himself. It turned out Chloe felt the same.

'She just wasn't right for him. Too shallow. All appearance and no substance.'

Yep, the claws were out.

'So is Alfie okay?'

'Yes, he realises she wasn't worth any grief. Besides he's back on duty from this weekend.'

'Back to the Navy?'

Chloe nodded. 'He's being posted somewhere overseas. We don't know where, but he'll tell us when he can.'

'I hope it's not Northern Island, bless him. It always seems scary over there with all the bombs and the IRA and everything.'

'No, it's further than that. We'll wait and see.'

'You'll miss him, Chloe. We all will. He's a lovely young chap. Very popular.'

'Yes, he is!' she giggled. 'But he'll be back again soon, and we can have another party. Any excuse for a party!'

Louise had a lot to tell Jayne and Toby when she rang them that evening. She told them about poor Dr Achebe and about Alfie too.

Everyone was sad about Alfie going away, but they were all quite pleased to hear Samantha had disappeared.

'Poor Nora though,' remembered Louise. 'She won't have any visitors again. I do feel sorry for her.'

'There's your sewing,' reminded Jayne, 'you can always go over and ask her for a lesson. You've still got her book, haven't you? Take her that pencil case we're making in Needlework and get her to help you with it or something.'

Louise wasn't thrilled with the idea, but thought it was something she should probably do.

'Think of it as your civic duty!' urged Jayne.

'My charity work!'

It was soon Valentine's Day. This was a big deal for Louise this year! She'd had cards from her parents when she was a little girl, but this was the first time she was sending one! She had nipped into the newsagents one day and bought a nice card, not too mushy, just a simple 'To my boyfriend' on the front with two cartoon dogs cuddling. Inside it just said, 'with love' and she had signed it. She knew tradition dictates Valentine's cards are anonymous, but she thought that was silly. She wanted Toby to know who had sent it!

It was a Sunday, so she took Olga for a walk and tentatively knocked on Toby's door, the card in her pocket in case his parents answered. But no, it was Toby, he'd seen her walking up the street. They were both a bit embarrassed but exchanged cards and hugs.

'I'll come out with you, if you like?' he offered.

'I'd like that.'

'I told my parents about you.'

'Oh?'

'They saw the card I bought you.'

'I see.'

'They weren't surprised, to be honest. They said I go on about you all the time!' He laughed shyly.

'Yeah, I think I'll tell mine later. I'll put the card up on the mantlepiece, they're bound to ask questions!'

As they walked along the street, Toby slipped his hand into his.

'What if anyone from school sees?' she asked him.

He shrugged. 'I don't care. We're official now my parents know.'

She smiled and held his hand tightly in hers. She didn't care if anyone saw either.

Book club soon came round again. Sandra was enjoying *The Great Gatsby* and that evening, they were going to discuss other famous American writers they had read and what they had thought to them. She was looking forward to giving Steinbeck some stick for *The Grapes of Wrath* - that grey novel of dust and dirge she had struggled with.

Brenda and Ruth were back, and Beatrice turned up too, so Sandra went to chat to them during the refreshments break, telling them how Louise and Toby were now 'officially' girlfriend and boyfriend. Martin (who she'd been sitting with) walked over to introduce himself to Hugh, extending his right hand in front of him. It was received warmly, and they exchanged friendly smiles.

'Hi, I'm Martin Smith. You're Hugh Stephenson, aren't you? I've been trying to work out where I recognize you from and it's just come to me, you're –'

Hugh put his index finger to his mouth. 'Please. Don't say anything. I moved here to get away from all that fame and gossip and tabloid oppression. It nearly ruined me. I love the anonymity of village life. I'm kind of in hiding, you see.'

Martin recalled the many newspaper articles from a decade or so ago. He remembered Hugh had quit his career due to serious problems with addiction and depression. Oh yes, he could understand that himself - the need to get away, to forget your past, to hide in a whole new world, a blank canvas to reinvent yourself.

'I understand, mate,' he said, touching him on the arm. 'Your secret's safe with me.'

Sandra came over with two coffees. 'Oh hi, Hugh. Sorry I didn't get you one.'

'Oh no, it's fine, thanks. I always carry water with me, so I won't die of dehydration.'

Belinda brought the meeting to attention, so everyone at down again in their original places. 'I'm pleased you've met Hugh,' Sandra commented to Martin, *sotto voce* so as not to incur Belinda's wrath. 'I think he's a bit shy. And probably lonely. He lives on his own with his two dogs. It'll be nice for him to make another male friend.'

'Yeah, we'll have to form a club. Single dog walkers. A bit like a Lonely Hearts' Club, but for bachelors with canines.'

She giggled. Belinda turned to her. 'Did you have something to add to the discussion of American writers, Sandra?'

God, it was like being at school. At least she could take her annoyance out on John Steinbeck!

Finally, Louise went round to Nora's to return *The Beginners' Guide to Sewing* book which she'd had since before Christmas. She had found it very useful. She also took the pencil case she'd made at school - a plain blue fabric with rows of different stitches across it which they'd had to practice. Louise rather enjoyed Needlework and was thinking of taking it as an option in the Third Year, when they could drop some subjects to concentrate on others, ready for O-levels.

Nora was pleased to see her and offered her a glass of lemonade, sitting down to admire the sewing on the pencil case. 'Can you put the book back for me, please?' Louise did as she was told. 'If you want to look through the others, you're quite welcome to borrow another one.'

'Oh thank you.' She began browsing through them, finally noticing one about making soft animals out of felt. 'This looks interesting!' She showed Nora the front cover. 'Have you ever made any of these?'

'Yes, I made lots for the family – dogs, cats, horses, I think I even made a dragon once for my grandson. Not much call for them nowadays though.' She sounded sad and Louise tried to cheer her up, chatting away about her pets and how she'd like to make toy versions of them.

'Your Lady Olga might be awkward to do with all those colours. Start with something simple, then add more in as you get used to it, as you get more confident.'

She took the book off Louise and flicked through the pages. 'Here,' she said, opening the page out to show her young visitor. 'These are easy to start off with!'

'Little ducklings, they're cute!'

'And you just need yellow felt, nothing too complicated. Look in that sewing box over in the corner there.'

Louise hadn't noticed it before, it was at the side of the chair but quite low down, so it wasn't obvious straight away. She opened up the lid. It was full of all sorts – threads in many colours, different sized needles in plastic containers, metal and china thimbles, a sewing enthusiast's delight.

'Bring it over here if you can carry it and I'll sort some bits out for you!'

It wasn't heavy, just a bit bulky, but Louise brought it over and Nora rifled through it, picking out some bits and bobs. She soon amassed a little kit for Louise, putting it in a small see-through bag for her. Then she added two big pieces of bright yellow felt. 'There you go, that should start you off nicely. Take the book with you and come back with a couple of ducklings. You could make them for Easter, give them to the doctor's two little boys, maybe. Then we'll see what you can do next. That should be straight-forward enough, the book's got pictures and good instructions, but if you get stuck, just pop over. I'm sure we can sort it out.'

Back at gym club the next evening, the gymnasts were listening to their coach speaking about the competition and how he felt they had dealt with the pressure. He was increasing the number of his top group to twelve and they would be his competition squad that he expected to train at least four times a week. As he read out his list of names, the girls waited nervously. Cally, Louise and Jayne had all made the team, but afterwards, Mr. Barber asked those three to stay behind.

'Now, because you girls are behind in your bars work, I want to get you to concentrate only on bars for the next two weeks, to get you up to the same level as the others who have been here longer. We have been very lucky to hire the expertise of a Soviet expert on bars – Lidia Chernova.'

Louise gasped. She had read about her in her gym books and magazines, she had competed in the 1970s and just missed making the USSR team for the 1976 Olympic Games. She would be bringing her autograph book to training! Cally and Jayne didn't seem to recognize the name, by their lack of reaction. Mr. Barber continued without pause.

'The British Amateur Gymnastics Association have been very lucky to secure her services for six months and she is travelling around the country, visiting different clubs and helping girls on bars. She arrives tomorrow night and I expect you three to be in the gym for nine o'clock on Saturday morning, okay? Bring a packed lunch and plenty of water, it'll be a long day. And don't forget your handguards!'

'Thanks!'

The girls were all thrilled. Even more so when Louise explained the pedigree of their guest coach.

'Let's hope our parents don't have too many plans for the next two weeks!'

Later that week, ITV started showing repeats of Hugh Stephenson's *Small Satires* show. Martin looked at the TV guide in dismay. 'Oh no!' he said out loud. He knew how the Press worked, anything to rake up scandal and gossip all over again. He realised this would be a catalyst to bring Hugh back into the public eye – the last thing the poor man wanted.

Sure enough, the week after the TV show was repeated, one of the tabloids published an interview with an "unknown source" – allegedly one of the crew of *Small Satires*. HUGH'S DRINK AND DRUGS HELL was one headline, while another of the scummy newspapers (as Martin thinks of them) speculated why Hugh quit television and where he is now, using the alliterative front cover headline of SMALL SATIRES STAR STILL STONED?

That night is book club. Martin really hopes Hugh is fine and will turn up, maybe have a little laugh with Martin quietly about how stupid the newspapers are, publishing such shit. He sits with Sandra and is obviously preoccupied, because she asks him what's wrong. Twenty minutes after the book club has started, Martin whispers to Sandra 'We have to go, it's urgent, I'll explain on the way.'

'Sorry,' he calls out to Belinda. 'Family crisis.'

In the five minutes it takes them to walk from the village hall to Hugh's house, Martin fills Sandra in on who Hugh is and his previous issues. She had vaguely heard of Hugh Stephenson but hadn't seen his programmes and certainly was unaware of his addictions. She agreed Martin was right to be worried.

As they got to number 11 Whitlock Close, Martin knocked on the door loudly, but only heard the dogs barking somewhere out the back. Sandra walked across the grassy front garden and peered in through the window.

'Martin! Quick! I think I can see him!'

They put their hands above their eyes to see better. There appeared to be a figure slumped half off an armchair in the back room.

'Get Dr Achebe!' Martin yelled at her, going to the front door and trying the handle, then kicking it as hard as he could.

The Doctor had been sitting in the lounge watching a film, so he came out straight away, grabbing his medical bag from the hall. He added his weight to Martin's, and they eventually managed to get the door off its hinge enough to break through. The two men rushed over to the figure.

'Ring for an ambulance!' the Doctor told Sandra, pointing to the telephone on the coffee table. She did, while the men went to Hugh. The Doctor checked him over.

'He's breathing, but shallowly and his heart rate has dropped. He's unconscious and he's vomited. Looks like an overdose to me. Whether intentional or accidental, I don't know, but hopefully we got to him in time.'

Luckily an ambulance was in the village, visiting a suspected heart attack patient who thankfully had just experienced a scary panic attack, nothing life-threatening. As they were putting their equipment back in the ambulance, they got the call through and headed straight for Whitlock Close.

Once Hugh was off in the ambulance, Dr Achebe by his side, Martin rang a locksmith to sort out the broken front door and Sandra went to check the dogs in the garden. Sooty and Sweep were friendly enough, but she couldn't have them to stay overnight with her dog and cats.

'I'll see if Nora could manage the dogs until Hugh's better. She's only next door, after all.'

She went to Nora's, knocking loudly. Of course, she didn't need to, because Nora's nose had been pushed up against her front window for the best part of half an hour.

'What happened? Who's ill?' She greeted Sandra.

'A hello is more normal,' she thought, but what she said out loud was 'It's Hugh, he's been taken to hospital. Is there any way you could look after his dogs until he's home? He's got two black Labradors called Sooty and Sweep. They're as friendly as anything, but I don't want to put them with other pets and most of us here have cats and dogs or lots of children.'

'Oh, I see,' she thought about it. 'Well, I used to have Labradors years ago. I couldn't take them on long walks, but I'll have them here and see how they get on. Just for a couple of days?'

'Well, hopefully, Nora.'

'Okay then.'

'I'll come to his house with you, and you can meet them, then we can bring over their bed, food, bowls, whatever.'

'Okay,' she said. She was actually starting to feel quite excited. She could do something to help her neighbour and it might turn out to be fun!

So Sooty and Sweep moved into Nora's and were spoilt rotten.

A couple of days later, Martin and Sandra visited Hugh in hospital. He was embarrassed, very sheepish and could hardly meet their eyes.

'I don't know whether to thank you or say sorry or what,' he said quietly.

'We're just pleased you're okay, mate,' Martin replied as Sandra nodded in agreement.

'It was just too much. You know. The TV show, those fucking tabloids. Sorry.' He looked at Sandra. 'I couldn't cope.'

'I know. We understand.' She held his hand lightly, hoping to offer comfort.

'Are my dogs alright?' he asked suddenly.

'Yes, they're great. Your next-door neighbour Nora is looking after them and they're all having a whale of a time!'

'Oh, that's a relief.' He paused then, looking up at them both. 'They've offered me one to one counselling. And medication. So hopefully I will get by. And no more drink or drugs.'

'We're here for you, mate. You're not on your own.'

'Everyone's been very worried,' continued Sandra. 'No one's criticizing you, we all have our own demons. We all just want to help, everyone in the Close really. A lot of people care about you.'

'Well, that's lovely to know.' He coughed to try to get rid of the lump in his throat. 'I guess everyone in New Barnham knows who I am now.'

'It doesn't matter, Hugh, they'll get to know you as a person, the more you get out there. They'll see you're a nice bloke.'

He smiled at them both.

'Besides,' continued Sandra. 'You won't be the most famous person in the village for long.'

'Oh good! Why not?'

'Sarah's moving her boyfriend Mark in and he's in The Unflappables!'

Hugh looked a bit lost. Martin explained 'It's a big pop band, they've cracked America and are now coming over here.'

'Ah, I see. Excellent! An old TV star can't compete with a young pop star. I'm happy to relinquish my title!' He laughed and suddenly looked much younger.

'Trust us to move into bloody Hollywood!' giggled Sandra. 'We'll soon be the only house without a celebrity in it!'

'Until your daughter makes the Olympics!' commented Martin.

Dr. Chidi Achebe received a phone call that week. It was from Dr. Millhouse, his boss at the village surgery.

'I was wondering when you could come back?'

Chidi was unsure of the words he had heard and asked for them to be repeated.

Dr. Millhouse explained further. 'We have had quite a few telephone calls these past few days, as word of your heroism has got round the village.'

'Oh, I see. You mean with Hugh Stephenson's overdose?'

'Indeed. In fact, one of your critics was in Reception just a few hours ago and was asking where 'that wonderful quick-thinking doctor' was. Apparently she has got over her, erm, shall we say prejudice, and specifically wants you to check her waterworks – her words, not mine – as she's having some problem with them.'

'Oh, I can't wait! Chidi laughed, finally feeling like he could breathe easily again. He knew his shoulders had been up near his ears with stress, but he purposefully rotated them now so they were back where they should be.

'Are you okay to start again Monday?'

'Of course, Dr. Millhouse, thank you.'

'I'll put your favourite patient in at nine o'clock then,' he said.

Chidi could hear the smile in his boss's voice. 'That will be perfect. I'll look forward to it.'

By the time Hugh was home, he had a new front door and many more friends. Everyone in the Close made an effort to say hi to him in the street or pop round to see if he needed anything. He was incredibly grateful. In fact, this outpouring of support and friendship had made him cry more than once.

He was especially grateful to Nora, who had lovingly taken care of Sooty and Sweep and was obviously sad to be parted from them. He told her she could pop round any time she wanted to see them.

'It's been so lovely having dogs here, Hugh. I'd forgotten how they make a house a home. I mean, I'm not fit enough to walk big dogs anymore like your two, but I'm thinking of getting a little one, a terrier or something.'

'I think that's a lovely idea,' he said.

A few days later, he knocked on Nora's door. 'Oh, hello love!' she said.

'I've got you a little something. To say thank you for the dog minding.'

'Oh, I told you, it was a pleasure.'

'Well, even so, I've got you a little present.'

He went to his car and came out carrying a small basket. Inside it was a little Yorkshire terrier.

'I rang the rescue centre to see if they had a dog that would be right for you. This is Tilly, she's eight years old and has a bit of arthritis, so she can't go on long walks, but would love a home with a back garden to play in and someone who's got the time to give her loads of attention.'

Nora found her eyes were full of tears and she couldn't speak, but she gave Hugh a big hug which said everything. They walked into the house, and he passed the basket to her, and Nora looked straight into the dog's eyes. It was instant love. For both of them.

Hugh made another couple of trips to the car, bringing in dog food, bowls, a dog bed, some toys, blankets, bones, even poo bags.

'Everything you need, hopefully. If I've forgotten anything, let me know. This is her favourite dog food, so she should be fine with it.'

Nora had taken Tilly out of the basket and was holding her. Tilly looked into her new owner's face and started licking away the happy tears that were there.

March 1982

The Achebe family were enjoying life. They felt happy in their new home, and they had all made friends. Beatrice and Sandra were close pals now, while Chidi had made a point of seeing more of Hugh. Of course, they were neighbours, and he liked the man, but there was another agenda too – as a doctor, he wanted to keep an eye on his mental health. Prevention is better than cure, he really believed that and this time, he hoped to spot any signs early if Hugh was descending into depression, so he could get it sorted before anything bad happened again.

Raymond and Noah had settled into primary school, Faith and Grace into secondary school. Beatrice wasn't worried about Faith, she knew she could take care of herself, but she still fretted over Grace sometimes. She still seemed so little, so shy. She had a good group of friends though, which was really important, and she was thrilled Grace was back into her sports again.

The following day, Grace competed in the Inter-School Cross Country Championships. New Barnham Secondary School sent a team of ten – a boy and a girl from each year – and the P.E. teachers. The first-year boy competing was Charlie Cook, so they were sat next to each other on the coach. He was one of the 'in' crowd, good looking, tall, confident and athletic. He was the kind who had always excelled in sport and expected to win everything he entered. He was like one of those American runners you saw at the Olympics who were devastated to win 'only' a silver medal. Grace had little time for that kind of attitude, and he was so wrapped up in himself that they sat in silence the entire journey.

When they got there, there was quite a lot of boring stuff to go through first. The teachers were checking registrations, the competitors were told a few rules and regulations, then they had half an hour to take refreshments or warm up for the event.

Grace didn't know any of the other runners, so she contented herself with some people-watching. Charlie was chatting up some girls from another school. She rolled her eyes. If they wanted a boyfriend like that, good luck to them. When she started looking for boyfriends, she knew she was more interested in their minds than their faces.

Meanwhile, there was great excitement in Whitlock Close, as a big white moving van had arrived at number five with Mark's belongings. Well, great excitement from Sandra, Chloe, Mabel and Nora anyway, who were all observing from different viewpoints around their houses and gardens.

Sandra felt an urgent need to check if her washing had dried yet, just as the not unpleasant looking Mark Thomas drove up in his flash car, a couple of minutes behind the van. She folded a couple of T-shirts up and slowly took them back inside, having a good old nosy as she did. With excellent timing, she reached her back doorstep just as Mark got out the car, which meant it would have been impolite not to go and say hello.

'Ah Mark, welcome to Whitlock Close!'

'Sandra, how lovely to see you again and thanks.'

He really was rather handsome, she had to admit. After smiling for a minute, she couldn't think of anything to reply, so she floundered. 'Better get these inside!' she said, indicating the dry clothes.

He nodded. 'Catch you later!'

'Well, his arrival had certainly improved the view!' she told the dog, who wagged her tail in agreement.

The runners at the Inter-School Cross Country Championships were well on their way. The weather was ideal, and the top athletes were making good times. Each runner wore a tabard to show which school year they were in, so Grace had a yellow one on. This made it easier for the officials to sort out times for each age group, as there were several parts to the competition – winners for each year, both male and female, plus the overall individual winners, male and female, then all the scores were added up to find the overall winning school. There was a lot of Maths involved!

Grace was quite happy, she was 'running her own race' as she had always done, since her P.E. teacher in Birmingham had noticed her potential and began coaching her, though back then, she ran shorter distances, but the advice still applied. Grace was really enjoying Cross Country - the fresh air, the views of nature and having time and space in her head to think – or to zone out, whichever she needed to do.

She had just passed the three-mile marker when she heard a shout of pain ahead of her. She ran in the direction of the noise and found it was Charlie Cook, his yellow tabard contrasting with the green of the grass and the red of his knee.

'What have you done?' she asked him, though it was obvious by the cut and the blood.

'I slipped. Hit some gravel.'

'Yes, that cut's pretty nasty, it needs bandaging.'

She thought quickly, then took off her shoes and socks.

'What are you doing?' he asked.

She used one sock to clean the wound as best she could, then wrapped the other one tightly round his knee as a bandage. Then she put her shoes back on.

'Can you stand up now?'

He could, if he leaned on her. He was much bigger than she was, but they managed. He flexed his knee. 'Well, it does feel a bit better, thank you.'

'Doctor's daughter,' she grinned at him. 'Just keep an eye on it. There's no blood coming through, so hopefully it'll be okay. Can you walk?'

He could, though only slowly and favouring his good leg.

'You'll need to go to the First Aid station as soon as you get past the finishing line,' she told him. 'It might need a stitch and it'll definitely need a proper clean up.'

'Oh thanks, you've been great. What's your name?'

'Grace.'

'Well, Grace, you go off and finish the race. Run for both of us!'

'Will do. Take care, Charlie!'

He hobbled off slowly in the direction of the finishing line, while Grace jogged to start off then increased her speed as her body got warmed up again. She was soon out of sight.

Another mile or so and Grace could see the finishing line coming up. She could see one or two yellow tabards in front of her, so she knew she wasn't going to win, but she hoped she would do enough to be selected for future races.

There were several teachers at the end, taking numbers, names, times and positions. Others were cheering them on, especially the runners that were struggling by the end and needed the extra encouragement. Grace hadn't found it too much of a struggle and completed the race well, not needing to collapse in a heap as many others had done. She just slowed her pace, took some deep breaths and walked over to the yellow base to give her details.

Two of the teachers from the other schools looked on admiringly.

'Well, that little black girl still seems relatively fresh!'

'Good time too, by the looks of it and only a First Year.'

'Did you notice she was running without socks though, just trainers?'

'Yeah. Must be an African thing.'

'Perhaps they don't have socks over there.'

Beatrice was waiting for her daughters to get home. Unlike many of the women in the Close, her attention hadn't been on the interesting new arrival moving into number five, but on wondering how her youngest daughter was getting on in her race.

She waited for her at the door. Both girls ran over and gave her a hug.

'Well?' she asked Grace. 'How did it go?'

'Oh, pretty good.' She walked in and threw her bags on the floor, leaning back on the sofa. 'The school came third out of eight schools and I finished third in the first-year girls, so….' She opened a zip pocket in the side of her navy P.E. rucksack and brought out two bronze medals. 'I won these!'

Beatrice came over, pulled her up into a standing position and proceeded to jump round with her in a circle on the front room carpet, Faith joining in. They were all smiling and laughing. They sat down a few minutes later, Beatrice catching her breath. She was a big woman in her late forties and not used to jumping around too often.

'Put them on then!' she nudged her daughter, who did. 'Ah, don't you look great! A real star!'

'I'll go and get the camera,' Faith said, running upstairs.

'Yes, we'll finish the film off on photos with the medals, then your dad can put it in for developing next time he's at the chemists. We should get the photos back next week, hopefully!'

Grace smiled. She loved her medals, her first ones for Cross Country, but she hoped they weren't going to be her last. She had really enjoyed the race, apart from poor Charlie. She'd seen him being patched up by First Aid earlier and he had waved at her, so she guessed he wasn't too badly hurt.

Peter Davison was proving to be a good Doctor Who. Despite Louise's initial reservations at 'her' Tom Baker being replaced, she soon accepted the Doctor looked different and enjoyed his stories. She especially liked the Cybermen. To her, they were much scarier than the Daleks. So she really enjoyed the story *Earthshock* and even talked to some of the kids at school about it, as she'd been so impressed.

Rob was proud of his daughter. She'd got most of her television tastes from him. They both enjoyed watching British sitcoms together, like *Butterflies, Hi-de-Hi* and *Sorry!* They also loved watching *Carry On* films, when they were shown on television. Sandra found all that stuff rather too silly and would much prefer to watch something about Lady Diana! In some ways, he and his wife were very different.

The village book club had another good turnout. Ruth and Brenda were back, so Sandra sat next to Brenda and when Martin arrived a couple of minutes later, he sat next to Sandra. This time, as they were still reading the set book for the month, they decided to have a discussion about the books they remembered and loved from childhood. Afterwards, they all said what a fun discussion it had been! So many books, so many precious memories.

Some of the older men there loved the Biggles books by Captain W.E. Johns and Richmal Crompton's *Just William* series. There was a lot of praise for Roald Dahl from many readers there, particularly for *Charlie and the Chocolate Factory* and *James and the Giant Peach*. Talk of the latter veered off into discussing the TV version from a few years before and Belinda had to pull the conversation back to books.

There was a lot of love for Enid Blyton, especially *Malory Towers* amongst the women, and *The Famous Five*. They had an interesting chat about the longevity of these books, Sandra commenting that her own daughter had a collection of around eighty Enid Blyton novels, although had already outgrown some of the titles for younger children like the Amelia Jane series.

They all had a good time throwing out book titles, authors and childhood memories associated with visits to the library.

'Do you remember the *Ant and Bee* books?'

'*Mrs. Pepperpot*!'

'*My Naughty Little Sister*!'

'*Black Beauty*!'

'*Ballet Shoes* by Noel Streatfeild.'

When it was time for refreshments, Brenda and Martin went to get the teas and coffees, leaving Ruth and Sandra together.

'I know it's not my business,' began Ruth hesitantly. 'But be careful of Martin.'

'What do you mean?' She frowned.

'Well, it's obvious he fancies you. He can't take his eyes off you. And I don't know why, but I don't entirely trust him.'

'He seems nice enough to me.'

'But he hasn't been here long, we don't really know him very well. There's just something a bit off about him. I can't really explain it.'

Sandra looked at her in a way that showed she was quite irritated. Ruth continued, 'Look, I'm sorry, I just don't want one of my best friends getting seduced by a serial killer or something!'

'I'm not likely to run off with anyone. I'm married, you know that.'

'Yes. Just be careful, that's all I'm saying.'

'You left Ken.' She tried to keep the accusing tone out of her voice, but barely succeeded.

'I did, and I'm much happier with Brenda than I ever was with him. But I did lose Bryony.'

They stopped talking as Brenda and Martin came back with the drinks, but Sandra stayed quiet and distracted for the rest of the meeting.

That weekend was Mothers' Day and the Thorpes had a big family dinner out at a restaurant together. As well as the three of them, Louise's Nanna and Grandma were there plus her aunts and uncles. They all enjoyed big family get-togethers and especially when they meant a nice meal out somewhere, meaning no-one had to do the hosting. Louise's mother was forever moaning about entertaining at home, because of all the hassle catering, being the hostess then tidying up afterwards.

Her cousins were all busy elsewhere that day, so Louise was the only child, and it made her feel quite grown up for some reason. She had made a Mothers' Day card at school for her mum and bought her flowers out of her own pocket money. She wasn't known for her ability to save up, so this was noted and appreciated by her mother! She also made two special cards for her Nanna and Grandma on Mothers' Day. She enjoyed drawing and designing things, though more often than not, the drawings would have something to do with gymnastics.

In the Achebe house, they also embraced Mothers' Day though Beatrice still insisted on doing the cooking! As well as making her cards, Faith had bought her a brightly coloured necklace and the four children performed a special song for her, which they had been practicing in secret. As usual, all happy occasions in their family were celebrated with lots of big hugs and happy tears!

In Sarah and Mark's house, they were celebrating too, though in a low key and rather cautious way. But, fingers crossed and all that, next year's Mothers' Day would be very special for them. By then, they should have their own baby! But it was early days, they had only found out a week before after Sarah had been to the Doctors for a pregnancy test. They weren't planning to tell anyone else for a few weeks yet, just to make sure. But they were both very excited.

Louise, Jayne and Cally were enjoying the extra sessions training on the asymmetric bars with Lidia Chernova, but they felt they had never worked as hard. When they had a five-minute break for a drink of water and a wee, they stood talking about their new guest coach.

'No wonder the Soviets win everything!' sighed Louise, taking a long drink.

'I know! I've lost count of how many repetitions we've done this morning.' Jayne was breathing deeply.

'I'm going to be doing these moves in my sleep!' moaned Cally.

All too soon, Lidia was clapping her hands, the signal for them to all go back to her and start training again.

'Okay,' she said, in her heavily accented English. 'Now, you girls' [she pronounced it 'geells'] – she nodded at each one, assessing their levels of fitness after the first session. 'You have all done the first parts very well. Now I want you to work on routines. Not just one element, two elements – but routines. So, try five to ten moves, it can be all easy ones, but together. I give you five minutes, you can have pen and paper if you want, to make notes.'

Louise made a list of all the moves she could do on bars and tried to link them together. Mounting on the low bar, dismounting from the high bar, with moves to travel between the two. She thought she could do a routine, it was just remembering which order was the best one.

Jayne had come up with something too – at least on paper. Cally was pacing around, looking fed up. She hadn't taken a notebook or pen.

Lidia was staring at her, sensing defiance. 'Cally! What is the problem? Why you no write routine?'

Cally turned to face her. They were the same height. 'I don't want to learn boring routines of these stupid basic moves. I want to do something exciting.'

'Like what?' Lidia had her hands on her hips now and her chin tilted upwards to make her slightly taller.

'A Radochla?'

Lidia laughed. It wasn't a friendly sound, more of a sarcastic one. 'You do bars five minutes, you think you do Radochla, yes?'

'Sure, why not?'

'Do you even know the mechanics of it? The preparatory steps you need to do?'

Cally was becoming more daring and ruder. Louise and Jayne were shocked to see this side of her.

'No, why don't you show me?'

Louise gasped. You don't talk to a former Soviet gymnastics star like that!

All three girls gasped next though, as Lidia removed her tracksuit and revealing a pretty pink leotard underneath, she launched into a bars routine which was beautiful and fluid and included a perfect Radochla – a straddle catch-and-release skill from the low bar to catch the high bar. She dismounted with a back somersault to a perfect landing. The girls were speechless. What a beautiful display and Lidia had been retired five or six years! She put her tracksuit back on and continued speaking as if nothing had happened.

'Louise, you go first.'

Louise began with a simple mount on the bottom bar and although her movements were slow and cautious, she got through it.

'Yes, that's good!' Lidia applauded her. 'You did nice moves and good rhythm. Okay, try to remember it. You write it down, yes?' Louise nodded in response. 'Good, read it, picture it, try again soon.'

Next was Jayne's turn but then Cally refused to practice, complaining she had a bad stomach and needed to go to the bathroom.

In half an hour, they had their hour lunch break. The girls took their packed lunches to the kitchen and ate them there, then went back into the gym to wait for Lidia.

'She's late!' complained Cally, looking at the big clock on the wall.

'Not by much. Let's just warm up a bit.'

Louise and Jayne began doing gentle warm up exercises – jogging round the floor, then little stretches, jumps, sequences of split leaps across the diagonal of the floor mat and building up to the basic moves.

Cally wouldn't join in.

The other two ignored her. They weren't going to ruin this special chance of being trained by a champion! Louise and Jayne were in the far corner of the mat helping each other stretch their hips, when they heard the creak of the bars. They turned in the direction of the apparatus, to see Cally doing an improvised routine, with no one there to supervise.

'Bloody hell!' said Louise, as they stopped doing their warm-up and ran over towards her. At the same time, the big doors of the gymnasium opened, and Lidia walked in with Mr. Barber. As they saw Cally on the bars, they quickened their pace too.

Meanwhile Cally was preparing to do a Radochla. She'd show them all what she was capable of! She released the lower bar in straddle. It wasn't too high up to the high bar, but it did take precision, timing and endless practice. No one expected to catch it on their first try! Cally reached to the high bar but missed it by a few inches, crashing down between the bars, landing on her neck.

Louise and Jayne were first on the scene, but Lidia yelled 'Don't touch her!' and Mr. Barber went off to ring for an ambulance. 'If she has injured her neck or back, it can be worse if you move her.' Lidia explained, gently checking Cally over, without moving her. She was talking softly to the injured girl but received no response.

The ambulance arrived in a few minutes, securing her neck in a brace and taking her off on a stretcher. She was still unconscious. Louise and Jayne both felt a bit sick. Mr. Barber left to follow the ambulance, ringing Cally's parents on the phone in the reception area before he left.

Louise and Jayne stood there with Lidia for a short time, but then Lidia took charge.

'Okay, girls, back to warm up.'

'But – you surely can't expect us to keep training, when Cally's hurt herself.'

'Why not?' The girls didn't answer. Lidia's voice softened and she sat down on the mat, getting the girls to do the same. 'Listen. When I was in USSR team, all the time girls got injured. Sprained ankle, broken arm, whatever. If one girl injured, do other girls go home? No. Other girls train. You're gymnasts, is what you do. When Olga Sherinova broke her hand at World Championships, she was first up. All girls had to go next. I did same vault, a Tsukahara. She fell and broke her hand. I landed it, was okay. It's sad about Cally but you don't waste time, don't waste your chance, yes?'

The girls nodded. It made sense when she explained it like that.

'Okay. Warm up now, then we go back to practicing bars routines. But – no Radochlas!'

Louise and Jayne smiled and began to jog around the outside of the forty-foot square mat.

The next day, Sandra rang Cally's parents to find out how she was doing. Thankfully she hadn't broken anything, the doctors told her she had been lucky. When she put the phone down, she filled in Louise on the details.

'She's got concussion and will be in hospital a couple of days for observation, but she's had X-rays and doesn't seem to have any broken bones. The doctors want her not to do gymnastics for a few weeks, just to check her neck and everything is fine, but they're not too worried.'

'Oh, that's good news. I'll pop round and tell Jayne.'

'Aren't you going to ring her?'

'No, I'll take Olga for a walk at the same time. I might see if Toby's in too.'

It suddenly all made sense to Sandra, who turned away from her daughter so she wouldn't see her grin. Young love. So sweet. She took some cups into the kitchen.

'Okay but I'll be doing tea for five o'clock, so be back by then.'

'Will do, Mum!'

'And don't forget the poo bags! We don't want Nora reporting us to the police for not picking it up!'

April 1982

Louise, Jayne, Toby and Grace had formed a lovely close group at school. They walked to and from school together and socialized afterwards. Robert had even taken the four of them to the April Fair, which they'd loved. They spent their school lunchtimes and breaks together too, but not today. Louise and Jayne had a gymnastics practice at lunch, because Mrs. Leighton wanted to put on a display for some visitors in the coming weeks and Toby had his chess club.

Grace was a bit bored. She'd eaten her school meal and taken as long over it as she could. Then she'd had a wander round their part of the playground but hadn't seen anyone she really knew and liked. She wished she'd bought a magazine to read but hadn't realised her friends were all busy at the same time today. She looked at her watch. Only twenty minutes to the bell. She decided to do another circuit round the school grounds. Well, it was better than just standing still for twenty minutes looking lost. As she turned round the corner of one of the blocks, she almost literally walked into Natalie, Suki and Tara from the Second Year. Oh no! She smiled politely and continued walking, but they stood in her way so she couldn't escape.

'Hey, look!' said Natalie, 'if it isn't our little African girl!'

Grace decided to try to stick up for herself, like her father often urged her to do. 'I'm not African, I'm English, I was born in England. I've never even been to Africa.'

'You can't be English with skin that colour,' sneered Suki. The other two laughed.

'Look at us! We're English, proper English and we're all white.'

'Yeah. And your hair's all funny too, kind of thick and wiry' added Tara.

'Don't you ever brush it?' Natalie caught a section of Grace's hair in her fingers and started twisting it. 'If you're not gonna look after it, maybe we need to give you a little haircut. What d'ya reckon, girls?'

Suki and Tara nodded keenly. 'Shall I go and get the scissors, Nat?'

Suddenly a male voice cut into their conversation. 'I think not!' It was Charlie Cook. He elbowed his way between the girls and Grace. Although he was a year younger than Natalie and her gang, he was taller and stronger than them and they knew it. They also knew he had an older brother, Darren, who was in the Fourth Year and would soon be after them, if they tried to have a go at Charlie. They started backing away, mumbling something about needing to check their make-up before classes started again. Charlie grabbed the sleeve of Natalie's blouse and pulled her back towards him. The other two followed like the sheep they were. He looked them straight in the eye.

'Listen to me, girls, because there are some things you need to know. 1 – This girl is my friend and you do not, I repeat NOT, bother her. Don't even go within five feet of her. 2 – You are nasty little racists and nasty little racists are worthless little shits. 3 – You're not worth any more of my time, so get lost. But remember what I said.' They turned to go, but he called them back. 'After you've apologised to Grace for upsetting her.'

They were literally squirming. And not rushing forward to apologise.

'Oh, it's okay, I'll tell Darren and he can catch up with you later, if you'd prefer?'

'Sorry Grace,' Natalie coughed out and the other two followed.

'Right, now get out of my sight and don't you dare repeat this behaviour again, do you hear?'

They nodded, then ran off. The bell rang for the start of afternoon lessons.

'We'd better go in, Grace.' He looked at her and saw she had pent up tears glistening in her eyes. He reached a tissue out from his trousers pocket and gave it to her. 'It's clean!' he reassured her.

'Thank you,' she squeaked.

'Hey, you helped me at that Cross Country race. One good turn and all that…'

They started walking back to the block their classrooms were in.

'Look, Grace, I was wondering if you'd like to go running with me sometimes after school? Or at weekends? If you're not busy?'

She looked up at him and saw him beaming down at her. Maybe he wasn't the arrogant cocky sod she'd thought he was. And it was only running after all.

'Yes. Thanks,' she said. 'That'd be nice.'

It was Lidia's final session with the girls at the gym club. They were going to miss her. After their training, they had a 'de-brief' where they went through all they had learnt from her and made notes about what they wanted to learn in future and how to practice each move in stages. As the three of them were sitting round the mats and it was quite an informal chat, Louise decided to be brave and ask Lidia something she could never dare ask her male coaches.

'When you were training and competing, what happened when you had your period?'

'In what way?'

'Well, I hate just wearing a leotard in case you can see anything, you know? My pad, or if I leaked or something?' Her cheeks were the colour of blood as she spoke.

Lidia nodded. 'Oh yes. Our coaches let us wear tracksuit bottoms while training, there was no pressure to just train in leotards. Can't you talk to Mr. Barber about it?'

Both girls laughed and shook their heads.

'Oh no, we wouldn't dare,' said Jayne.

'And Jayne, you have same problem as Louise, yes?'

She nodded shyly.

'Okay, I talk to Mr. Barber. Don't worry, I don't say your names, just that in USSR, we have girls training in tracksuit bottoms if they wish. I say, "women's problems", he ask no more!' They all giggled together like little girls. It was easy talking to Lidia, she was like a big sister.

'And in competition?' Louise asked her.

'Ah yes, coaches give us contraceptive pill, you know? You take them for some days, you no have period. After competition, you stop pills, you have period. Easy.'

'Over here, we have to go to the Doctors to get those pills and we need to get our parents' permission if we are under sixteen.'

'Oh okay. I can get some for you. I give them to your coach before I leave.' She saw the girls' horrified faces. 'Don't worry, it will be plain bag. I say is little presents for my girls, yes?'

'Thank you.' They both gave her a big hug. Yes, they would definitely miss her and not just for her incredible coaching.

Chloe came over to the Thorpe's house that evening. She wasn't her usual self at all. She was quite subdued, accepting a coffee instead of requesting one, sitting down quietly, perched on the edge of the sofa rather than sprawling across a seat and a half.

Sandra settled down on her favourite chair, cup in hand, dog on her lap. 'Are you okay, Chloe?'

'No, not really.'

Usually at this point, Chloe would be talking for England with Sandra lucky to get a word in. Instead, there was silence for a few minutes, then Sandra tried again. 'What on earth's wrong?'

'It's Alfred.'

'Yes?'

'Have you been watching the News?'

'No, not really, why?'

'Have you heard about the Falklands?'

'Oh, the Argentina thing? I heard something on the radio news this morning but didn't really pay attention.'

'Yes, Argentina have invaded the Falklands Islands, claiming it's theirs, when it's British.'

Sandra shrugged. She still didn't understand what this had to do with her or Chloe.

Chloe persisted. 'We've just sent in a Naval Task Force.'

'Oh.'

'Alfie's on it.'

Now Sandra understood. She looked at Chloe, noticing how pale she looked, how her hands were shaking so her coffee was close to spilling over. She reached across the room, put the cup down safely on the table and gave Chloe a hug.

'Oh God, I'm so sorry, I didn't realise.'

'It's all hush-hush, we're not supposed to know.'

'You heard from Alfie?'

She nodded. 'No details, of course, he just said where he was.'

'But he's been in Northern Ireland, he knows what it's like.'

'Yes, he has, Sandra, but this is a whole new situation. How much do we know about Argentina?'

'Evita's from there? Julie Covington sang that song…'

Chloe frowned. 'Exactly. Nothing. I'm really worried, San.' (She let that one go without comment.) 'He's my little boy.'

'I know, I know.'

Robert walked in five minutes later to find them hugging, Chloe sobbing in his wife's arms. They hadn't heard him, so he backed out the front door and decided to go and check on Hugh. He'd leave the women to their women's things.

Hugh was pleased to see him. He had regular visitors since he'd come out of hospital – Gerry, Martin, Chidi, even Nora once with the dog! At first, he'd found it difficult in some ways, knowing these people were aware of his weaknesses, the demons he was constantly fighting. But he had slowly relaxed, realizing they weren't coming into his home to pry, or to leak a story to the press. No, they were friends. They simply wanted to be there, to help, and he loved this cul-de-sac for that.

He put the kettle on, Rob following him into the kitchen.

'Thanks for coming over, Rob. I appreciate it.'

'Well, actually, you're doing me a favour.'

'Oh? Why?'

'Well, I got home and found Chloe Smallacre sobbing in my wife's arms. I felt they didn't want me there, right at that moment.'

'So, you thought you'd come and see how the old depressive's getting on?' He laughed.

'No, I was going to come over soon anyway. It just ended up being sooner than I'd thought.'

'Only teasing you, mate.'

Rob took the cup of coffee from Hugh, and they went into the lounge to sit down.

'I don't know what's up with Chloe though,' Rob continued. 'Never seen her cry like that before.'

'Oh shit, I've just had a thought!'

Rob looked at him eagerly.

'Is their lad in the Army or the Navy?' asked Hugh.

'Royal Navy.'

Hugh checked his watch, it was six o'clock. He turned the television onto the BBC News. The first item was about the Falklands conflict.

'This!' he said. They listened to the item in silence. The reporter was listing some of the British vessels involved. 'Is Alfie likely to be on any of those?'

Rob shook his head and shrugged. 'I only know he's in the Royal Navy. Nothing else.'

'Well, it's unlikely to be a coincidence, is it? Neighbour's crying on your missus and her lad's in the Navy.'

'Yes, you're right. I hope he's okay.'

Nora was watching the same news coverage, cuddling Tilly anxiously. She loved Alfred like her own son and had a bad feeling he would be in the Falkland Islands now. She felt God had deserted her years ago, when her husband died and her life fell apart, but that evening, she prayed to God again, to keep Alfred safe from harm. Just in case there was a God after all.

Cally hadn't returned to City Gymnastics Club. Rumours were that she had changed clubs, but Louise and Jayne hadn't even seen her at school, so they didn't know. They thought her pride had been injured as much as anything else and she must feel embarrassed, the way she behaved.

The special bars training sessions were over, and Lidia Chernova had moved on to work at a gym club in London where a couple of members of the British national squad were coached. The girls knew she'd be an asset, especially as the British team weren't particularly strong on the bars.

Meanwhile there was another competition coming up, this time against the Leicester girls, who were also a strong team. Mr. Barber told the ones he'd picked to compete that they would have extra training at the weekend, where they'd be expected to show their full competition routines, just as if it was actually the event. Then the coaches would make comments to the girls as to where and how they could improve. This would give them another week of training to work on the weaker parts of their routines before the actual competition.

Louise and Jayne were really excited, knowing their bars routines had improved so much under Lidia's guidance that they would be able to score much higher this time around.

'We just need Olga Korbut to turn up to help us on beam now!' Louise joked to Jayne.

They had been working on new moves and Louise was struggling to get her back walkover on the high, four-inch-wide balance beam. She tended to twist to one side, then miss the beam with one foot. She knew losing 0.5 for a fall wouldn't help her climb the rankings. Oh well, she knew gymnastics wasn't an easy sport!

Mr. Barber handed them the package from Lidia, explaining it was 'some sort of present for you both. You really made an impression on her, you know.'

'Ah she's fab, we loved her!'

The two girls took the package to the toilets and opened it where no one could see them. Inside were some packets of contraceptive pills along with instructions on how to use them. She had also enclosed signed photos for each of the girls and a couple of little gold USSR gymnastics pins, plus her address so they could keep in touch.

Sandra heard a knock on the door. She looked at the clock and saw it was only quarter past ten, so too early for the postwoman who usually came in the early afternoon. She opened the door to find Martin standing there.

'Oh hello!' she said. 'Fancy seeing you here!'

'I've been visiting Hugh.'

'Oh, how is he?'

'Good, yeah.'

'Excellent.'

She didn't know whether to invite him in, but after Ruth's comments at Book Club, she wondered if people would talk if she did. And she knew Nora's curtains would be twitching right about now.

'I was wondering if you fancied bringing Lady Olga out for a walk.'

She looked at his empty hands. 'But you haven't got Scamp with you.'

'Holy missing dog, Batman!' he said in a fake American accent. 'I know, I'll get him on the way.'

She considered what she had planned for her morning and realised it was only the ironing and that could wait.

'Yes, why not? I'll just get the dog saddled up and I'll be right with you.'

He dutifully waited on the doorstep, but she got ready quickly and they walked out the Close together. As Sandra walked past Nora's, she gave a quick wave and was rewarded with a swift hidden movement, as the curtain moved back into place.

'Caught ya!' Sandra said to herself, gleefully.

It was the first time she had been in Martin's house. It was fairly small, but there was only him and the dog, so she guessed he didn't really need anything bigger. She didn't go upstairs, but it looked like a two-bedroom. She went into the kitchen to get a glass of water while he got Scamp ready to go out. He had the kitchen, lounge and dining room downstairs, all standard square rooms. He didn't seem to have much out on display to show his tastes. Sandra always loved looking at people's record collections, book collections, videos, family photographs – all the sort of little details that told you things about the person living there. But there was nothing like that here. How strange.

Soon he had got Scamp ready, she finished her water and they were out walking the dogs in his end of the village. She usually took

Lady Olga around her estate or to the village park, which was only across the road from the village hall. She didn't venture up this part of New Barnham very often, but she knew Jayne lived a couple of streets away and Cally was on this estate too with her parents.

They walked in silence first, watching the dogs interact with each other, doing a lot of sniffing. Soon Lady Olga and Scamp realised neither were a threat and they happily toddled alongside each other, just stopping for a wee or a smell of something or a half-hearted growl at a cat across the road.

'It's good they get on well,' commented Sandra.

'Yes, they seem to remember each other from last time. Scamp's good with other dogs though, he's not an aggressive sort at all.'

As they continued to walk further into the fields, Sandra realised the conversation wasn't flowing as well as it normally did when they were together. In fact, she was feeling slightly awkward, though she didn't understand why. She decided to make an effort and find a safe topic to talk about.

'How are you getting on with the book club choice?'

'Really good, I've read it before, but it's always good to go back to an Agatha Christie. I never remember whodunnit!'

'I'm the same! I enjoy them too, although I do prefer the Miss Marples to the Poirots.'

'You see, I'm the opposite, though Margaret Rutherford was brilliant in the old films!'

'She was! I didn't see any bookshelves in your house, don't you read much?'

Martin laughed, though there wasn't much humour in it. 'You been judging me by my possessions, or lack of?'

She tried to laugh it off. 'Oh, I just noticed when I was at your house. I like seeing what authors people read, that kind of thing. I think possessions can tell a lot about people.'

'That's why I don't have any.'

She didn't know if he was joking or not, so she left it hanging, without comment.

A couple of minutes later, he continued. 'I keep my books in my bedroom, especially the ones I'm currently reading. There's a small pile on my bedside table. A few in the spare room too. I tend to keep things away really.'

She usually felt perfectly at home in his company, like she had known him for years and trusted him completely. Today, she didn't know why, but it was a different kind of atmosphere, and she wasn't entirely happy, and she definitely wasn't relaxed. Her shoulders were tense, she could feel them. Making a conscious decision to take a couple of deep breaths and calm her increasing heart rate, she ostentatiously looked at her watch.

'I think we'd better turn back, my mum's going to ring in about half an hour. I just remembered.'

It was a lie, she usually rang her mother, not the other way round. The reasoning was that Sandra was more likely to be out and about, although her mum did go shopping once a week and still went out dancing one evening a week with her friends. Anyway, Martin didn't know any of this.

He looked at her a bit strangely but shrugged and they turned back retracing their steps. 'Well at least the dogs will be happy.'

'Yes, Olga's a bit fed up with cats, living with two of them. It makes a nice change for her to socialize with another canine!'

'We can definitely do this again, can't we? It's been nice.'

Sandra made a noise which she hoped was neutral enough. At this point, she didn't want to commit either way. She was definitely feeling uneasy and as wanted to be back home, without this man. Back home, indoors, with the doors locked. Safe.

As they got to the village green, she said to him 'I'll cut back via the path near the school, it's a bit quicker. I'll see you later.'

'Okay,' he said. 'I need to pop into the Co-Op anyway. See you later.'

She walked away from him, heading home, every footstep making her feel slightly happier.

Even back at home, sitting on the sofa with a cup of tea, she couldn't understand the feelings she had, it seemed completely irrational. But they were there, nonetheless.

Gerry was trying to comfort his wife. He'd got in from work to find her watching the News, cuddled up in a ball on the sofa.

'You must stop watching it, love. It just makes you worse.'

'No, I need to know what's happening over there. What it's like for him.'

'You weren't this bad when he was in Northern Ireland.'

'No, I know. That was nearer, the Falklands are so far away. And this is a war, Northern Ireland was more – I don't know – peace-keeping?'

'This isn't a war. It's a conflict.'

Chloe spat out a 'Pah!' noise. 'Call it what you want, people are dying, and our son is over there.'

'I know. I understand your worrying but try not to. We'll hear from him in a few days, you'll see. Besides, this Falklands thing will be over soon.'

He went to put the kettle on, praying that he was right, and everything would be okay.

Louise and Jayne were thrilled, they had done all their competition routines and performed well. Mr. Barber and the other coaches had been full of praise for them, especially for the improvement they had shown on the bars. The competition against the Leicester gymnasts required City Gymnastics Club to send two teams of six girls – an A team and a B team and both girls had made the A team. They were so excited! They couldn't wait for Mr. Thorpe to pick them up, so they could tell him the good news.

May 1982

It was seven o'clock in the morning when Sarah Willington heard an unearthly wailing. She was getting ready for work and waiting for the cafetiere to finish dripping, but the noise set her on edge. She couldn't place the sound at all. She opened the side door and looked out. The noise was coming from the Smallacre's house next door. She could see lights on in the front room.

She pushed her feet into her slip-on shoes and went to their front door. She had to knock a few times before she was heard, then a very shocked looking Gerry opened the door.

'Is everything okay?' she asked, suspecting it wasn't. 'I heard a noise -'

She saw behind Gerry that there was a figure on the carpet, curled up in a tight rocking ball and the sound was emanating from there.

Gerry ushered Sarah out of the house and quietly closed the door behind them, whispering 'It's Alfred. We've had some bad news.'

'Oh my God! I'm so sorry to hear that. What's happened?'

Gerry was fighting to hold it together, to keep his composure, but Sarah could see he was struggling. 'Look, you go and look after your wife.' She said, 'I'll get the doctor.'

Wordlessly, Gerry did as she was told, while Sarah ran to number nine, where Beatrice answered.

'Is the doctor in? There's a crisis at the Smallacre's! It's something to do with Alfie.'

'Oh no!' she put a hand on her chest, then crossed herself. 'Chidi! Quick!'

Her husband ran downstairs, hearing the urgency in his wife's voice.

'What's wrong?'

'It's the Smallacres, Dr. Achebe. I think something's happened to their son. Chloe is beside herself. Literally on the floor and crying.'

'Okay, thanks Sarah.' He picked up his medical bag and hurried to number seven, knocking before letting himself in.

Beatrice saw how pale Sarah looked. 'Hey girl, I'm just having a coffee. Want one? You look shocked.'

Sarah nodded. 'Yes please. Oh Jesus, I hope their son's alright.'

'Me too, honey, me too.'

It was over half an hour later when Chidi came back home. Sarah had finished her coffee, thanked Beatrice and gone home to finish getting ready for work. Her car had left Whitlock Close just a few minutes ago.

Chidi came in and sat on the sofa as though he'd done twelve hours of manual labour and was physically exhausted.

'Are they okay?' his wife asked.

He shook his head, took his glasses off and rubbed at his eyes. 'No, they're not. Alfred's dead.'

'What?'

'He's in the Falklands Islands with the British Royal Navy. He got killed yesterday.'

Beatrice crossed herself again, shut her eyes and whispered a prayer.

'Oh, what an evil thing war is!'

He nodded in agreement. 'What happened?'

'They don't know any details. They had a phone call this morning giving them the basic facts.'

'How are Chloe and Gerry?'

'I've given Chloe some tranquilizers, she wasn't coping at all, could hardly walk, had problems breathing. She was close to having to go into hospital, but Gerry said he'd look after her and I've promised to go back after work tonight.'

'How's Gerry?'

'Stoic. Putting on a front.'

'Do they need anything? I mean, I could go round after the kids are all in school.'

'No, I think they'll be okay. Gerry wants me to go and tell the Thorpes and Nora though. They need to know, and he couldn't face doing it himself.'

'I'm not surprised! Poor man! That poor family!'

Dr Achebe felt like he'd done a full day's work even before he walked into the village surgery. It had been hard breaking the sad news to the Thorpes and even worse telling Nora. Robert had kept his composure, hugging his wife and daughter to him as they began sobbing. The doctor advised them, in his medical capacity, to keep

Louise at home today, to ring in and explain the circumstances to the school.

Nora was inconsolable. He made sure she was sitting down when he told her, but she seemed to shrink into the sofa afterwards, as if her bones had turned to jelly. Even Tilly couldn't comfort her and Chidi hated leaving her alone, but he had to get to work. In the end, he asked Mabel next door if she'd go and sit with Nora, explaining that poor Alfred Smallacre had been killed and Nora was taking the news very badly. Mabel agreed straight away, and he drove off to work, knowing at least the old lady wouldn't be on her own.

At first Nora couldn't see anything. Her eyes were blurred with tears, her throat sore from the deep sobs coming out of it, her heart aching for the young man she had known most of his life. But then she registered another presence in the room with her. She wiped her eyes on the sleeve of her cardigan and as her vision cleared, she saw it was Mabel. Standing in her room! The cheek of it!

Mabel spoke first. 'I'm sorry to intrude, Nora. Dr Achebe came to see me. He said he didn't want you to be on your own. He had to go to work. I'm so sorry about Alfred, I know how much you loved him.'

Nora couldn't do anything but nod. Her voice wasn't strong enough to speak and she had lost all her words anyway. She was out of fight, out of anger. She had no energy to do anything or say anything. Sitting upright was difficult enough.

'I'll put the kettle on, Nora. Make us a cuppa.'

How futile that would be, thought Nora. Would a cup of tea solve the world's problems? Would it make everything better? Would it bring Alfie back to life? Rewind time and make it all fine again? Everyone heads for the kettle, it's the done thing. But why? She didn't understand it. She just knew that, tea or no tea, a part of her heart, her being, had died the moment Alfred had been killed.

Sandra was watching the BBC News when Robert came in from work.

'Quick! Sit down! It's about Alfie.'

There were photographs on the TV of the men killed on the attack on the HMS Sheffield. The reporter was explaining what had happened. 'On May 4th, the Type 42 destroyer was attacked by Argentinian Exocet missiles.' Recorded images were shown of the ship being hit in the middle and catching fire, smoke billowing into the sky, as the reporter continued to speak in his most serious voice. 'There were 281 crew members on board. Twenty died in the attack and twenty-six were injured, mostly from burns, smoke inhalation or shock. Only one body has been recovered.'

'Oh my God!' Sandra said. 'What if the body is Alfie?'

'What if it isn't? Which is worse?'

'Should I go to see her?'

'Last I heard, she was being sedated. I think it's best not to bother her at the moment.'

'It's so hard to know what to do. I don't want her and Gerry to think we don't care.'

'They'll know we're thinking of them. Chidi keeps going to check on them, he's all they need at the moment – and each other.' He gave his wife a hug. 'I'm so grateful Louise has had this gym competition to distract her. She's been training so much, she's not really seen the News.'

'Yes, she would have been struggling watching all this stuff. She really cared about him. I think she saw him as a sort of big brother figure.'

Indeed, Louise was focusing all her attention on the competition against Leicester. The contraceptive pills were working, so at least she didn't have to worry about getting her period during a competition now. This time, their families couldn't come along due to the small size of the venue, so the girls and coaches were cheering for each other instead. Louise and Jayne were warming up along with the other Team A members, while sizing up the opposition.

'You see that girl with the Olga Korbut bunches?' Jayne nodded. 'That's Lizzie Hall, she competed in the Champions Cup in January, I saw her on the telly.'

'God, we've got no chance!' wailed Jayne.

'Those two on the left are in the British team too – Ruth Hollands and Sarah Longman. Sarah's really good at bars, she got something like 9.50 at the British Championships.'

'Blimey, Louise, we might as well go home now, we're never going to beat them.'

'It doesn't matter. Compete against yourself. Improve your scores, hit your routines. That's what matters.'

'You'll be a great coach one day!'

'Ha ha, maybe, we'll see.'

They were watching Sarah Longman compete on bars. 'Wow! She's amazing!' said Jayne.

'Isn't she? Bet she's been on bars since she was a toddler!'

They applauded as she landed her shoot front somersault dismount beautifully. Then more applause for her score of 9.45. 'I'm just hoping to beat the 5.50 I got last time!' laughed Louise.

The City girls had already vaulted, all of them scoring in the sevens and eights, which was what they'd expected. They were next up on bars, following the success of the Leicester girls. Louise was feeling confident after her extra coaching from Lidia, and she was happy the routine was within her capabilities and one she could concentrate on performing to the best of her ability, with beautiful execution – straight legs and pointed toes, for example. Bars routines only last around thirty seconds and it seemed like a lot less than that for Louise, who found herself landing her dismount perfectly. She was thrilled. Mr. Barber and her teammates ran over to hug her. 'Great routine!' said the coach. She scored 7.90 and everyone was very happy. Jayne went up next and also gave a solid performance for a 7.80. All six girls in the City A squad did well, but nothing could compare with Leicester. Never mind, they could work towards higher marks, cleaner routines and no errors.

165

When it came to errors, Leicester showed their fallibility with five of the six girls falling off the beam. With its narrow width, it was always a precarious piece and although they had harder difficulty than their rivals, they made more mistakes and every fall lost the same amount of marks, regardless of what move they had been trying to complete.

City's first girl up, Ella Jones, was their eldest competitor at seventeen and she had been competing since she was twelve, so she was used to dealing with pressure and produced a good 8.65, which was a great start for the team.

Jayne was up after Ella and although she had a couple of wobbles, she didn't fall and was happy with her 8.00. The next two scores were in the low eights, then it was Louise's turn. She was trying a new combination of a back walkover into back flip, which she had only been completing about 50% of the time in training, but her coach had told her to try it anyway. It would gain bonus marks if she managed to do it successfully.

She mounted with a press to handstand, then did a line of dance, the compulsory full turn on one foot then prepared herself for the difficult two linked skills. Her coach and teammates watched her nervously, knowing this was a big moment for them all. She paused then went for it – and executed it beautifully, without even a wobble. That really encouraged her for the rest of the routine, as she knew her hardest bit was over. She landed her dismount with just one small step back and after presenting to the judges, she ran over to Jayne, who was jumping up and down with glee for her best friend.

'Great job!' said Mr. Barber, patting her on the back then turning his attention to the score board. 8.50, wow, so much better than the 7.30 she had earned on the beam in February.

The final girl up hit her routine for an 8.40 and the City team had gained some valuable points on the beam, compared to their rivals.

The floor exercise would decide the results. Both teams did well on this piece of apparatus, the top Leicester gymnasts even managing double twists and they all scored well with no falls or big mistakes. Ella Jones fell on her full twist, and they knew they had no chance of winning now, but Louise and Jayne both improved on their previous floor scores with 8.00 and 7.90 respectively, so they were satisfied.

They accepted their team silver medals with big grins on their faces, then stood in a line on the edge of the floor mat while the All-Around medals were announced, all of which went to Leicester. Thinking it was now over, the City girls began to move off, but the announcer continued. 'The medals for the top highest vault scores go to…' Not realizing there were apparatus medals up for grabs too, they shuffled back in line, hoping no one had noticed them moving off too early.

'On beam, the bronze medal goes to Louise Thorpe of City Gymnastics Club with 8.50.'

Jayne nudged her. 'Oi! That's you!'

Louise went off to the podium in a dream, standing on the Number Three step as instructed. She was dazed. She hadn't known about these medals and certainly hadn't thought she was up for any of them, even though many of the other team had fallen off the beam.

'The silver medal goes to Lizzie Hall of Leicester Gymnastics Club with 8.60.'

Lizzie had already won the All-Around competition and the vault. Even though she had fallen off the beam on her pirouette, she had landed some impressive acrobatic skills which pulled her score up.

'And the gold medal goes to Ella Jones of City Gymnastics Club with 8.65.'

They all cheered! It was the only gold medal for City, but they were thrilled with it, especially as the bronze was theirs too. Louise, Lizzie and Ella had the medals presented to them, then everyone cheered, and the announcer moved on to the floor medallists.

When Louise got home later that evening and walked into the house with a team silver medal and a beam bronze, her parents were thrilled. As soon as she'd finished telling them all the details, she rang Toby to let him know too, then her mum and dad rang their mothers and soon the whole family was celebrating.

Just for a short time, they forgot about the loss of Alfred and had something to smile about again.

Sadly the Smallacres were lost in their grief.

Chloe and Gerry were existing. They were breathing, they were moving (though not very far), eating and drinking - little, but enough to keep them alive. They hardly spoke to each other – for what was there to say? This new world was one where time ran its own course, they were only vaguely aware of day and night, sliding around each other like ghosts.

Gerry dealt with the basics on autopilot. The dogs were fed, the most essential of chores were done. Chloe mostly sat on the sofa staring at the telly, which was never turned on now, they couldn't bear it. And days clicked over into new days somewhere in the distance. But it didn't matter because nothing was important now. Nothing.

June 1982

Mabel was still popping round regularly to check on Nora. Although the visits had been awkward and tense at first, Nora was becoming more relaxed. She realised – albeit rather begrudgingly – that she did enjoy the company and it was very pleasant to be able to talk to another woman around her age. While she enjoyed seeing little Louise, she could hardly discuss her arthritic knees with a twelve-year-old!

Cuddling Tilly on her lap, Mabel was telling her about the book club at the village hall. 'You really should try it, Nora, everyone's very friendly.'

'I can't walk that far.'

'I'm sure something could be arranged. Maybe Hugh could drive you there when he starts going again.'

'I wouldn't want to put on him like that. He's already done so much for me, giving me Tilly.' The dog really had made such a positive difference to her day-to-day life, and she would always be grateful to him.

Mabel was persistent, but at least understood when to change tack before the women ended up arguing – again.

'Look, I know you like reading, Nora. How about I pass on the books we read to you, then you and I could discuss them here, have our own little book club?'

Nora sipped her tea. She thought about it and couldn't think of a reason to say no.

'Okay. Yes. Thanks Mabel.' Another sip of tea. 'That sounds a good idea.' But it hurt her to say it. She still harboured some resentment towards this woman. But why cut off your nose to spite your face? Overall, she had to admit, she was pleased to have a visitor. And she did think, if she was ever ill, it would be useful to have Mabel next door to look after Tilly.

'Brilliant! We recently finished an Agatha Christie. Is that your kind of thing?'

'It is actually, I still watch them when they come on the telly.'

'Great, I'll pop it over tomorrow then.'

June 8th was Robert's 37th birthday. It was a lovely day, the first proper sunshine of the year and his plans were to get home from work, eat his tea out in the garden then relax with his family, his pets and the latest *World's Fair* for the evening.

Every year, Sandra tried to persuade him to have a party. Every year, he resisted. Besides, this year, his best mate was grieving the loss of his son and even Sandra had to agree that was a good reason not to have a big birthday celebration. But he did agree to doing something for his 40th – the 'something' to be negotiated over the next couple of years.

To his surprise, he had a few visitors that evening. Hugh popped over with a card and a selection of beers but didn't stay long. Then about half an hour later, Chidi knocked on the door. He had his hands full. He handed over two cards to Rob, then two big bottles of whisky – one wrapped, one unwrapped.

He pointed to the one wrapped in sparkly birthday paper. 'This one's from me, Beatrice and the kids. Big Happy Birthday from all of us!'

'Oh thanks, that's really kind of you.'

Chidi pointed to the unwrapped bottle. 'And this one's from Gerry.'

'Gerry? Oh, bless him, I didn't expect him to bother. He's got so much on his plate.'

Chidi nodded. 'Definitely, but I went round to see how they were getting on and he asked if I'd mind bringing this to you. He can't face going out at the moment.'

'Understandably!'

Chidi nodded. 'So I told him it was no trouble as I'd planned to come and see you today anyway.'

'Thanks. How are they doing?'

The doctor sighed. 'Getting by. He's functioning okay, doing what he needs to, going through the motions. Chloe, not so much, she's still on medication. But it's early days, hopefully time will do its job and things will get better.' He paused. 'But let's not dwell on sad things. How about you open one of those bottles and we have a quick celebratory tipple? If I'm lucky, I might just miss the chaos of bathing the boys and putting them to bed!'

They had a giggle and Rob got the glasses. 'What I want to know is, how come everyone buys me alcohol? Do you all think I've got a problem?'

He poured out two generous measures of the whisky, they clinked glasses and sat down happily. Sandra had just nipped out to buy him a last-minute cake, Louise was at gym club, so the two men had at least half an hour's peace and they were going to savour it.

Two days later, he was still relishing that peace he'd had, just him and Chidi and the whisky. Sandra was now obsessing about going on the Village Twinning trip to France at the end of July. Rob was very happy to go, but not so keen to dive into the unknown territory that was the Twinning Committee. From what he'd heard, it was made up of a Stegosaurus, a Triceratops and lots of Tyrannosaurus Rexes. And he doubted Gerry and Chloe would be up to going this year, so he wasn't even sure he'd know anyone.

He came up with the old classic. 'Sandra, if you're interested in it, why don't you go?' but, as usual, she listed all the household chores she had to do, suggesting he was expendable, and she wasn't. Personally he suspected his go-out-to-work 'chore' paid the bills better than her washing-drying-ironing, but he kept his mouth shut because he didn't fancy having to iron his own shirts in the doghouse. Sandra's younger sister always said she could start an argument in an empty room – and she was right! He knew when to shut up.

So, heavy of heart, one Monday night, he entered the village hall for the Village Twinning Committee Planning Meeting and yes, it was as exciting as it sounded. Luckily they served strong coffee. He had hoped he could register an interest in the trip, fill out a form then head off home in time for some British sitcom on the telly. Instead, it all dragged on and on. He seriously struggled to stay alert and interested. He suspected the old men would make a Carry On film seem slow and boring. But without the cleavages.

He did get to fill in a form, but he had to be talked through it by Dick Rayner. How to explain Dick in a few words? Moustache, monotone, moron. Did he really think Rob had no idea what 'date of birth' meant? The trip was expensive too. They were allowed to pay in installments if they booked early, but with only a few weeks, they had to pay it all in one go. He mumbled something about 'checking with the wife' and escaped as soon as he could.

When he got home, Sandra said 'That took a long time! I was expecting you back an hour ago!'

'Me too! I'm exhausted. I need a whisky!'

'Well, you know where the glasses and booze are kept.'

He sighed. He was sure it wasn't that long ago that men were fussed over by their wives. Sandra had even talked about getting a part-time job and then what time would she be able to cook tea? Things seemed to be changing too fast. He got his own glass and poured out a double measure. What the hell!

School work was winding up as the summer holidays approached. They'd had the annual school trip to the Lincolnshire Show, where all the kids had come home with promotional bags, badges, hats and pens advertising local businesses. Now they were concentrating on the end-of-year tests. The pupils would be put in sets for the Second Year in September, so the results would be used to stream them, along with the teachers' own notes. Louise, Jayne, Toby and Grace were all good pupils and weren't too worried about the tests, though they knew things would get harder. Faith was always complaining how much homework she got in the Fourth Year, and they had been doing mock O-levels too.

It was the lunchtime after their first English paper and before their second Maths one. They were all eating in the dinner hall when Charlie Cook came in. After he'd got his meal, he came over and asked Grace if he could sit next to her. She smiled at him and nodded. Louise and Jayne gave each other questioning looks. Did this mean something?

After they'd all eaten, Charlie said 'I'll see you at five tonight then, is that okay?'

'Of course. See you later.'

'Bye everyone!' They all replied as he took his tray over to the stack of empties, then walked out into the playground.

Grace suddenly had three interested pair of eyes on her.

'Well?' Louise asked, too impatient to wait for her friend to start talking.

'What's happening at five?' questioned Toby.

Grace's embarrassment changed to pride in front of their eyes. 'We're going running together. You know, practicing for the next Cross-Country race.'

'Oh is that what it's called now?' teased Jayne. '*Running together?*' She laughed.

Grace stood up. 'Yes. That's what it's called. Because that's what it is.'

She took her tray over and walked out the same door as Charlie had, not even looking back at her three friends.

'Oops!' said Toby. 'I think we took that a bit too far.'

They nodded sombrely. 'Yes, think we better go after her.'

Grace hated being the centre of attention, even amongst her close friends. She had always preferred blending into the background. The only time she was fine with it was if she was getting positive attention for her sporting achievements. Somehow that was different. It wasn't her, it was her ability.

She had decided not to tell her mates about training with Charlie because she knew what they would say and they didn't mean it unkindly, but she didn't really bother with boyfriends and all that kind of thing. Since Louise became Toby's girlfriend, she could find romance in anything! Grace wasn't denying she liked Charlie and even admitted her initial impressions of him had been totally wrong, but at the moment at least, they really were 'just good friends' and she didn't want that to be sullied by gossip and rumours. With her religious upbringing, she certainly didn't want people to think her and Charlie were like Sabrina and Paul! She was happily traditional, even old fashioned and believed people should be much older and married before they even thought about sex! She was happy to stay a young girl in that respect, not grow up too quickly as far as boys were concerned.

It had been a while since Sandra had been over to Ruth and Brenda's, what with Alfred dying and so many things being put on pause. It just hadn't seemed right for her to go round to see her friends, laughing and joking like nothing had happened. But now she felt she was neglecting her friends and ought to get back to a bit of normality, so she'd rang them the previous evening. They'd been very happy to hear from her and she had arranged to go over this morning.

Ruth and Brenda were also friends of the Smallacres and were grieving over Alfie, but there was an unspoken agreement that the three of them should talk about something else instead. They did give Sandra a hug as she walked in though, then Brenda went into the kitchen to make the drinks.

'It's great to see you again, Sandra. I thought I might have upset you with what I said at Book Club about Martin,' said Ruth.

'No, not at all. In fact, wait until Brenda comes back, I'd like to tell you something. Well, ask your opinion really.'

Ruth was intrigued. Brenda brought through the hot drinks, placing them on the coffee table and her bottom on the sofa next to Ruth. They exchanged a few pleasantries about the weather improving and asked how Louise's gymnastics competition had gone. Then Ruth said, 'So you wanted to ask our opinion about something?'

Sandra explained how Martin had arrived on her doorstep and about going to his house. Ruth raised her eyebrows at that point. 'Oh God no!' reassured Sandra. 'Nothing like that. I stayed downstairs and absolutely nothing untoward happened.' Ruth nodded. She believed her friend completely.

'But his house is really strange. He didn't have any personal possessions on show. It was like he'd been there a week, not a year. We got Scamp and took both dogs out for a walk across the fields, but it was so weird. I just didn't feel happy. We weren't chatting away like we usually do. He was a bit, well, off, I guess. I can't explain really, it was just a feeling. But I made an excuse and left. Then at home, I shut the door and felt just, well, relieved.'

'Hmm,' commented Brenda. 'That does seem weird.'

'But, Sandra, you haven't known him that long. Have you met any of his friends or neighbours? Has he chatted to anyone when you've been out?'

'Well, he's friends with Hugh now, I'm not sure if he knows Chidi. He's never spoken to Rob or Gerry as far as I know. And no, I've never seen him talk to anyone apart from us lot at Book Club.'

'Yeah, I'd back off a bit, Sandra,' advised Ruth. 'Surely if he's been in that house a year or so, you'd think he would have made some friends or at least know people to say hello to.'

'I wonder if I could get Rob to ask around at work, see if he's come to the attention of the newspaper in any way. I just don't know what else to do.'

'You could ask his friends about him, but he doesn't seem to have any.'

'Just be careful, Sandra.'

'I will.'

'Next time he wants to go for a walk, come round here. Make up an excuse, say one of us is ill or something. We're usually in, you don't need to ring first.'

'Thanks Brenda, I will, that's very kind.'

'Not at all, just looking out for you. Don't want you getting abducted by a weirdo!'

Sandra stayed for a second coffee, and they began talking about summer plans. Ruth had been hoping to see Bryony in the school holidays, but Ken had told her they were going to Spain for a few weeks, and he'd let her know when they were back, so it was all vague and Ruth wasn't holding out much hope in seeing her.

'So you've not got any holidays booked then?'

'No, Sandra, what about you?'

'The three of us are going on the Village Twinning trip to France next month for a week. Rob went to the planning meeting and filled in the forms, so we've just got to write the cheque.'

'Oh that sounds interesting, I read the notice on the village hall noticeboard, but thought it'd all be old blokes in their seventies wanting to go and see where they fought in the War!'

'Oh, it is!' Sandra laughed at Ruth's quite accurate description. 'But we're going too. I don't know if other families from the village are as well. The Smallacres usually go, but -'

'It might be an idea for us, Brenda. We haven't been to France for a few years, have we?'

'Do you go by coach, Sandra?'

'Yes, coach and ferry.'

'So we could have a rest from driving too. Hmm, sounds a good idea. Where do we get more info from?'

'Rob's got the organiser's name and number. I'll ring you when I get back and let you know.'

'Brilliant! This could be fun!'

'It'd certainly be better if you two went as well!' Sandra said happily.

On the way home from school, Louise was talking to her friends about the trip to France too. Toby was especially interested. 'My parents are always talking about going to France and visiting those old War sites, I wonder if they might be interested in the village trip. Is it full?'

'No, I don't think so. Dad said there weren't that many at the meeting, mainly the usual old men you see selling the poppies around the village.'

'I might ask them about it then. Wouldn't it be great if we could go too?'

'It'd be fab, Toby! What about you, Jayne?'

'I think we've got our holidays booked. We usually have a couple of weeks visiting family, then two weeks in Wales or somewhere. I'll have to check, but I don't think they'd fancy taking Harry on a really long coach trip. Can you imagine those old boys moaning if Harry was crying all the time?'

'Yeah, I bet they're not very tolerant when it comes to kids making a noise.'

'Oh yes, Louise,' teased Toby. 'You'll have to be seen and not heard for the entire trip!'

She hit him with her school bag, and they chased each other round the village green for a couple of minutes, before calming down.

'I'll mention it to Mum tonight, Louise and let you know.' He said, as they separated to go to their homes.

Before her husband went to work that morning, Sandra asked him to have a look through his newspaper archives to see if the name Martin Smith came up anywhere.

'Is he that guy from Book Club, who visits Hugh? The one that you were with, the evening Hugh was ill?'

'I wasn't *with* him, Rob, that sounds dodgy. We were at Book Club together. But yes, that's the one.'

'What do you think he might have done?'

'I don't know exactly. Maybe nothing. Hopefully nothing! But I was talking to Brenda and Ruth, and we were saying how he just turned up at Book Club out of the blue and none of us really know him.'

'You turned up at Book Club and no one knew you!'

'Yes, I know, but I don't have a questionable past.'

'Neither does Martin, as far as we know.'

'Well, just look, okay? He's been in the village nearly a year and doesn't seem to talk to anyone except a few of us from Book Club.'

'Yes, I've made a note of the name.' He put away his notebook, indecipherable shorthand all over it. 'But it won't be the first thing I do today. I do have proper work to do as well. We've got a VIP function with Princess Margaret soon and we need to work out all the timings for that.'

'Okay, just see what you can do.'

She kissed him goodbye.

It was gone midday, no wonder she was hungry. She'd done her housework then got into a new book she had been lent by her sister. She'd have to take Lady Olga for a walk too, unless she could persuade Louise to do it after school. There was a knock at the door. Probably the postwoman, she thought. They had two or three post ladies in the village, which was good. I mean, why not? They had all been men in Lincoln.

She opened the door wide to find it was Martin standing there. Before she could find her voice to say anything to him, he walked into the house, causing her to move aside for him to get past.

'What's wrong?' he asked.

'What do you mean – wrong?'

'You've been avoiding me. And I just saw Ruth and Brenda in the Co-op and they were funny too.'

'I've no idea what you're talking about. Shall I put the kettle on?'

'No need.'

She felt trapped. She didn't have an excuse to go into the kitchen, so remained standing awkwardly in the middle of the front room.

'Sit down!' he told her, not too politely. She did, though she wasn't sure why. It was her house after all. Shouldn't she be telling him to sit down? He did anyway. He perched on the end of the sofa facing her. The pets had all disappeared, she noticed.

The phone rang and she jumped, then tried to laugh to ease the tension. 'I'd better get that.'

Martin didn't respond.

She picked up the receiver. 'Hello?' It was her husband ringing from work in his lunch break.

'Hi love. I've been doing a bit of digging for you. About that Martin bloke.'

'Oh. Yeah?' She hoped Martin couldn't hear her husband's voice.

'So, he was accused of beating up his wife in 1980. There're photos of her in hospital, black and blue, poor woman. But he didn't get charged. Had some alibi. Sounds like he had a mate who did him a favour, reading between the lines. Said they were at his house all evening drinking, that kind of thing. Police seemed annoyed, but they didn't have enough evidence. So it was dropped, no one else was ever charged. They split up and he moved away. Obviously we know where to.'

Sandra had no idea what to say. She was acutely aware of who was in the next room and needing to keep her voice calm, so as not to panic the man, especially now she knew why he had moved to the village. Even if he wasn't charged with assault, it sounded extremely possible he had done it.

'Are you okay, love? You've not said a word.'

She forced her voice to sound light and airy. 'Oh yes, it's just I've got a friend here. Don't want to leave him on his own for too long, don't want to be rude.' She laughed as best she could.

'Hugh?'

'No, it's Martin from the book club.'

The phone went down at Rob's end. Sandra pretended he was still on the line and continued to chat to the noise of the tone. 'Yes, he's fine, just came over for a chat,' she said to no one. 'Okay then, yes, no problem, see you later. Bye.'

She replaced the receiver, took a deep breath and walked back into the lounge, smiling her best acting smile at Martin on the sofa. 'That was Rob from work.'

There was a prolonged silence. She sat back down on the chair, trying her hardest to think what she should do. She knew Rob was on his way, but it was at least a fifteen-minute drive from his office, and anything could happen in that time. She had to act for her life here, she wasn't sure what this man was capable of, but he couldn't suspect she knew anything about his past.

'Have you been reading the book?' she asked him, desperate to find some neutral ground.

No! Listen, I want to know what's wrong with you. You've been avoiding me. Since that walk, when you came to my house.'

'I haven't, I've just been busy. It was Rob's birthday, Louise had her gym competition and now they've got exams. There's always something going on to keep me out of mischief.'

'So let's go to my house then, if there's nothing wrong.'

'Your house?'

'Sure, why not?'

'Well I've still got things to do here, get tea ready and everything, for when Louise and Rob get home.'

'You've got ages before the school day finishes. Come on, let's go to mine.'

He suddenly darted across the room and pulled her up from her chair pulling her arms with his hands. 'It's warm enough, you won't need a coat or anything. Just your house keys.'

She had to try to stall, to give Rob chance to get some way towards the house. If she left here, he'd not know where she'd be. He didn't even know where Martin lived! She only knew because he had taken here there with the dog that time. What the hell was she supposed to do?

'I need a wee first,' she said, heading towards the downstairs toilet.

'You can go at mine, it's only a few minutes' walk, your bladder's not that old you can't hold it in.'

She didn't like this rough, cruel side to him. She had been so silly to fall for his charm school act. But what were her options now? He pulled her out of the door and waited for her to lock up. When she fumbled with the key, he pulled her other arm back hard. He wasn't going to stand for any delaying tactics.

Her next plan was to wave at Nora, to try to indicate to her that she was in trouble, that she needed help. As she walked past her front garden, she waved, hoping her facial expression would give away her true fears. Nora waved back, apparently not noticing anything unusual.

If they saw anyone who looked like they could help her, Sandra decided to shout 'Help!' and take her chances. But he walked the back way to his house, through the fields and they saw no one. It was early afternoon, kids were at school, adults were at work or maybe at home doing something, but they weren't out in this part of the village. No one was there to help her. She had to sort this mess out herself. She couldn't rely on Rob saving her.

Mabel was feeling uneasy. She had seen Sandra go past with the man from book club and she hadn't seemed happy to go. She was convinced something wasn't right, but she wasn't fit enough to go in pursuit, and she could hardly ring the police! What would she say? 'My friend walked out of the Close with one of her friends.' It's hardly suspicious, certainly not a crime. But she wanted to do something.

She remembered that Belinda had handed out a list of Book Club members' phone numbers last time, following the incident with Hugh. She felt it was a good idea for the group to keep in touch and to be able to ring each other if they were concerned, especially as several of them were elderly and had health problems.

She ran her finger down the list, finally finding the number she wanted. She dialled it quickly and it was soon answered.

'Hello?'

'Ruth? It's Mabel from Book Club.'

'Oh hello, how are you?'

'Look, I'm worried about Sandra. It may be nothing, but she just left the Close with that man from Book Club. It may have been my imagination, but she didn't look happy to me.'

'Martin?'

'Yes, that's the one, I couldn't remember his name.'

'Which direction did they go, do you know?'

'I think it was left out the Close. They were walking.'

'Any dogs with them?'

'No! That's a good point. When I've seen them together before, they always had the dogs.'

'Thanks Mabel, you're a star. Don't worry, me and Brenda will go and look for them.'

Rob was driving as fast as he could. He hadn't bothered to explain anything at work, he'd just left. They'd be time to go through it all later with his boss. Now the only thing that mattered was getting to Sandra, before that violent lunatic did anything to hurt her. He knew the police were heading to New Barnham too, they were taking it very seriously and had assured him they would get on to it straight away, but he still felt he needed to be there too. Besides, the police had other priorities; he only had one – to get to his wife.

Sandra tried to walk as slowly as she could, but every time she paused or dawdled, he grabbed her arm and tugged her forwards. They were heading for his house, she could see it in the distance now. God knows what his plan for her was – if he even had a plan! He hadn't said a word to her for a while now. She was thinking how to play it, should she be defiant or compliant? So far, any defiance she had shown had been met with a violent response. She could feel bruises blooming underneath her skin where he had pulled her arms hard.

Suddenly she heard the two-tone of a police siren. Maybe it was coming to help her? But how would they know where she was?

The police car arrived at Whitlock Close, two men jumping out at number three, shouting and banging. Nora and Mabel both came out of their houses at the same time. They called one of the men over and explained what they had seen. Nora consulted her notebook and told him the time she had seen Sandra leave. Mabel told them she hadn't seemed to be walking willingly with Martin. Realising the Close wasn't where they needed to be, they got back in the car and followed the road in the direction Mabel indicated.

Rob got home about five minutes after the police had left. Nora and Mabel both came out and explained the situation to him. He got back in his car and sped off up into the village.

Ruth and Brenda knew vaguely where Martin lived. He had told them once at a book club meeting and Sandra had described it to them when she'd last been over, but they didn't know the exact number of the house. They guessed he'd crossed through the fields though and were following the likely path.

Brenda was flagging. 'I'm not fit enough for this, Ruth, you hurry ahead!'

Ruth began jogging in the direction of the houses past the field. Brenda stopped to take some deep breaths, then followed behind at a much slower pace.

Martin unlocked his front door and shoved her in. She ran straight to the back door, but it was locked, and the keys weren't anywhere nearby. He was blocking the front door.

'You won't get out. It's all locked up.'

She walked back into the hallway and faced him. 'I don't understand what I've done, Martin. Why are you so angry? I thought we were friends.'

'That's the problem with you women. You act all nicey-nicey at first, all flirting and promising things with your eyes, with your body language. Then you change.'

'I haven't changed, Martin.' She was trying to act in a friendly way, seeing if that tactic helped. She had seen that challenging him did no good and she couldn't see a way to escape.

'You have! You changed that day you came here. What was it? Too small for you? Not good enough for you? You're just like my ex, you are. Judging, judging, judging.' He put on a high-pitched girlie voice. 'You don't earn enough money, you don't work hard enough, you're not good enough.'

'I haven't said anything like that!'

'But your eyes did. When you came here. No possessions, you said, meaning I've got no money.'

'I didn't mean that at all. I was just wondering where you kept your books and records.'

There was a hard knock on the front door. He put his finger on her lips to tell her to shush. But she didn't. She screamed at the top of her voice. 'Help! In here!'

The door opened and Martin was kicked from behind, hard, more than once. He fell to the floor, leaving a gap between the front door and his body. Ruth's head popped round. 'Quick, Sandra, come on!'

She ran towards her friend, but as she stepped around Martin's body, he shot out an arm and grabbed her leg, pulling her off balance. As she fell, her head hit the bannister with a crack.

A two-tone outside. Ruth looked out. 'Here! She's here!' They came running over. 'Ring an ambulance!' she said urgently.

By the time Brenda had made it to the house, things were under control. The police had arrested Martin and put him into the back of the police car, handcuffing him with extra force and the odd kick. They didn't like men like him.

Ruth stayed with an unconscious Sandra until the ambulance arrived and they got her on a stretcher and into the back of the vehicle. Rob arrived just after that and he followed the ambulance, taking Ruth and Brenda's phone number and promising to let them know what was happening.

After everyone had gone, Ruth heard a whimpering from the back room. Walking in there cautiously, she saw Scamp locked in a cage, crying pitifully.

'Brenda, fancy a bit of dog fostering?'

They let him out, put his lead on and got a bag of his essentials together. As they left the house, Brenda locked up and pocketed the keys which had been left in the door. The two women headed back home, Scamp sniffing excitedly at all the new smells that had appeared since his last walk.

Robert rang Beatrice from the hospital to explain the situation and to ask if they could look after Louise until he got back from the hospital. She said she would be happy to do so, of course and said how sorry she was to hear about Sandra's experience. She was still unconscious, but the hospital staff were confident it wasn't anything too serious. Beatrice said she'd send Chidi over when he got back from work, to see if he could find out anything more.

Nora and Mabel were tutting together over cups of tea. They were coming out with all the tried and tested phrases.

'Well, you never know what's going to happen…'

'And on our own doorstep too.'

'You should never trust a stranger.'

'You can't be too careful.'

Of course Nora had sussed out Martin straight away! 'I knew he was a wrong 'un, as soon as I saw him. I even made a note of what times Sandra went out with him.' She failed to inform Mabel that she kept a record of everyone who came into and out of the Close, regardless of who it was.

Chidi caught up with Rob at the hospital. He'd spoken to the doctors there and they had confirmed what they had told Rob. They were keeping her under constant observation but felt she would soon regain consciousness. The scans had shown a small amount of bleeding on the brain, but it had stopped and was healing. It was just a case of waiting now.

'The prognosis looks good. They got to her straight away, so that's the best thing. Quick intervention. Are you staying overnight, Rob?'

'Yes, I think so, Chidi. Well, I'd like to. Would you and Beatrice be okay to have Louise all night though?'

'Of course, it's no problem. Do you want me to go and get you some spare clothes or anything?'

'No, I'll be alright for now, thanks. You couldn't feed the pets though, could you? They will be going mad on their own!'

'Not a problem at all, my friend,' he said, taking the house key Robert offered him. 'We'll have the dog overnight too, if you like.'

'That'd be great. The cats will be fine by themselves as long as they're fed. They use their litter trays anyway and don't go out at night.'

'Fine, don't worry then, Beatrice and I will sort everything out for you.'

'Thanks so much! You're a real mate!'

So a worried Louise and a happy Lady Olga slept on a spare mattress and sleeping bag on Faith's bedroom floor. Chidi had donned his Reassuring Doctor hat and had persuaded Louise that her mum would be fine, she might just take a couple of days to come round, because she had banged her head. The adults had decided not to tell her too much about Martin's involvement, she didn't need to know all the details right now. Anyway, he was in police custody, and they would be surprised if they saw him again, so there was no point making her scared.

At Ruth and Brenda's home, there was finally a tense kind of peace. When Scamp had first walked in, he has been so excited to sniff round a new place, then his excitement had hit puppy level to find there were lots of feline friends there too! The felines themselves had ranged from nonchalant to defiant to aggressive in their responses, but Scamp had his nose bashed a couple of times by inquisitive paws and hadn't retaliated, so they had come to accept he wasn't a threat, and the cats were back to their normal routine. Just as long as the dog didn't think he could sleep on the bed at night, that was their domain. He could have the sofa if he asked nicely.

July 1982

Sandra was back home and feeling much better. She was still officially resting and had a few headaches from her injury, but she was so pleased to be out of hospital and back to the Close. Everyone had been so kind, especially the Achebe family who had looked after Louise while Rob had stayed with his wife. As soon as she got back, Beatrice brought over several homemade meals to save them having to worry about cooking for a few days. Beatrice was an excellent cook and Sandra, Rob and Louise really enjoyed her food.

'I married the wrong woman!' teased Rob, giving his wife a hug. He was very relieved she was so much better. It had scared him when she was unconscious, but she made a quick recovery after the worry of the first twenty-four hours or so.

A couple of days later, there was a knock at the door. Rob had taken some time off work to help his wife, so he was there to answer the door. He was insisting Sandra took it easy and she was lounged on the sofa reading a book, Lady Olga by her feet.

It was Chloe at the door, but Rob had to stop himself gasping out loud at her appearance. Her pale skin and dark circles under her eyes aged her in a way the years might never manage. Her felt like giving her an impromptu hug, but she looked breakable and vulnerable, and he didn't risk it. Instead he forced a big welcoming smile on his face, told her how lovely it was to see her and invited her in.

She walked into the front room before uttering her first word. 'Sandra! How are you doing?'

One look at Chloe made Sandra reply 'Not too bad, thanks,' while trying to work out how to ask her neighbour the same question when she already knew the answer.

Chloe sat down on the chair, facing slightly to one side. Sandra could tell how much weight her friend had lost, her arms looked thin through the sleeves of her blouse. Rob brought the hot drinks through from the kitchen and sat at the edge of the sofa.

'I'm so sorry about Martin,' Chloe said quietly. 'I just wish I could have done something to stop it, you know.'

'He fooled everyone, Chloe,' said Rob. 'I guess that's just how people like that are. Manipulative, cunning. You didn't know him well anyway. He didn't talk to many people. Perhaps if you and I had seen more of him, we might have sussed what kind of a guy he was.'

Sandra gave her husband a look, which he missed. She let the comment pass, though did feel a sting at the implied criticism of her deductive powers.

They sipped their drinks quietly, each accompanied by their own thoughts.

'Oh I saw Mabel going round to Nora's this morning,' Rob came out with. 'I'm so pleased they are friends again.'

'That was Alfie's doing really,' smiled Chloe wistfully. 'He hated people falling out. He could see they were both lonely and unhappy…'

Sandra knew she had to say something about Alfie. She just didn't want to upset Chloe even more.

'That's very true, he was a good soul. How are you and Gerry doing?' she managed. Not very original, but heartfelt.

Chloe shrugged. 'We're still here.' She tried to smile, but it was a bit twisted, like a painter's brush had slipped and the shape wasn't quite right.

'We're so sorry,' Robert added.

Chloe nodded and finished the rest of her coffee in one big drink. 'I'd better get back.' She seemed to be trying to think of a reason, something she had to get back for, but failing to think of one, the sentence had to suffice as it was.

'Thanks for coming over,' Rob said as he walked to the front door with her. 'We appreciate it. And please tell Gerry we are thinking of him too.'

She nodded and wordlessly walked out the door. She headed directly to her house in a straight line, as if there was a piece of string between the two.

Rob shut the door, came back in and collapsed onto the chair. 'Jesus!' he said.

Sandra just nodded. 'What I've been through is nothing compared to them. Such loss. Mine is just a temporary blip. But their situation? They'll never get over it.'

Rob leaned forwards putting his head in his hands. Mitty jumped up onto the arm of the chair, pushing his black head against him for attention.

July 4th may be Independence Day in America, but in Whitlock Close, it was all about Faith Achebe's sixteenth birthday. The family had decided to have a big party for school friends the day before, as it was a Saturday, and the girls could sleep over. Then on the actual day, neighbours and family were celebrating together. The oldest of the five Achebe children – Emmanuel, who was twenty-six – was coming over as well, which was exciting for all of them.

Louise and Jayne were invited to both days, so they stayed overnight at the Achebe's house on the Saturday, sharing Grace's room with her. Faith's room was already full, with her four best friends from school staying. They had a lovely girlie evening, chatting, eating homemade food Beatrice had cooked and listening to music. Faith's friends had bought her some of the records she loved in the charts, so they played *Fame, Happy Talk, Iko Iko* and some of the other current hits, which they all loved. Everyone listened to the Top 40 and recorded it with their tape players!

The older girls taught the younger girls some make-up and beauty tips and they all had lots of fun. Faith and her mates were happy to include Grace, Louise and Jayne in their evening, they weren't the sort of girls who felt younger ones were beneath them in some way. As Faith explained, being the second oldest of five kids meant she was used to being around kids of different ages in her day-to-day life.

The girls all went back late Sunday morning, so the house could be tidied for the afternoon party. Louise and Jayne both had a nap, as they'd been awake most of the night.

Sandra was looking forward to meeting Emmanuel Achebe. Beatrice was always talking about him, and she was curious to know what he was like.

The party started at two o'clock in the afternoon and about an hour before, Mabel popped over to the Achebe's house. 'Sorry to interrupt,' she began, as Beatrice answered the door. 'I know you'll be busy getting ready. Nora and I can't make it this afternoon, but we have some cards for Faith.' She offered them to Beatrice, who thanked her and smiled. The old lady continued, in a whisper. 'There's some money in them, so keep them safe.'

'That's very kind of you, Mabel. Are you sure you won't pop in later?'

'No, I'd rather not. I appreciate the invitation, but I'm not really one for parties. But wish Faith a lovely birthday.'

'I will do. She's just in the bathroom getting ready, but I'll tell her, and I'll keep the cards safe too.'

By the time the Thorpes were all ready, it was quarter past two. Rob had been ready for a good forty minutes, of course, wearing the shirt his wife had ironed for him and a pair of plain black trousers. It was the girls who were fussing about their make-up, whether their outfits looked right, whether the shoes matched the clothes. Not only Sandra and Louise, but Jayne was there too. He felt decidedly outnumbered.

When they got there, they found the Achebe house was busy, noisy, colourful and welcoming. Bright banners and balloons decorated the house, and the beat of the music was thumping through the walls. Faith ran up to them hugging the girls, even though it had only been a few hours since she had last seen them. Sandra gave her a kiss on the cheek and handed over a card and a present wrapped in bright pink wrapping paper.

Not far behind her were Hugh, then Sarah and Mark. Everyone said hellos and happy birthdays and there were hugs, kisses and shakes of hands. The Thorpes walked into the dining room to help themselves to the buffet there, as instructed by Chibi. Rob was always happy to eat Beatrice's cooking, while Sandra was eager to seek out the one Achebe family member she hadn't yet met. Ah! There he was! Standing next to Grace, with little Noah holding the edge of his long purple shirt, as if he was scared his brother would go away if he let go.

Sandra went straight up and introduced herself. 'You must be Emmanuel!'

'Indeed I am.' He grinned a big handsome smile at her. He was tall, over six foot and slim.

'I'm Sandra from number three.'

'Oh yes, Mum's talked about you a lot.' He had a distinctive Birmingham accent that the other kids didn't seem to have. 'It's great she has made such good friends here.'

'Oh, she's lovely, your family have fitted right in.'

'Well, I'm pleased to hear it.'

Sandra called her husband over. He was balancing a paper plate filled with party nibbles. She introduced them to each other. Rob tried shaking hands, but it was too precarious with the food, and he ended up laughing, apologizing and just saying hello instead.

'I'm a big fan of your mother's cooking!'

'Oh, we all are! She makes the best food!'

Hugh came into the house. He seemed quiet and didn't meet people's eyes much, but he stayed for an hour or so and everyone greeted him and made sure they said a few words to him.

Sarah and Mark came over to chat to Sandra. She asked Mark how he was settling in and about his band. She didn't really know him well enough to ask anything else. Sarah talked to her about her job and how she was looking forward to the end of term, as she was feeling tired.

Sandra's brain was working at 78rpm. The tiredness, plus she had thought Sarah had put on some weight lately. There was normally nothing on her and now there was definitely a bit of a tummy. But Sandra's thoughts were silenced, before they had time to develop any further. The noise seemed to stop, and people hushed. Sandra turned round to see what was happening. Chloe and Gerry were walking in, holding a bag of something pink and pretty which they gave to Faith, wishing her a happy 16th.

'Wow!' whispered Sandra. 'I wasn't expecting them to turn up.'

'Oh, is that the couple from next door who lost their son?' Emmanuel asked in an even quieter tone.

Rob nodded. They watched as Chloe fussed over the birthday girl. Gerry spotted his best mate and headed directly for Rob. There was an awkward moment when they weren't sure whether to hug or shake hands, but they decided on a matey tap on the arm, which did the job.

'Pleased you made it, Gerry.'

'Well, we weren't sure, but she does need to get back out there. She can't stay home forever. It's not doing her any good at all.'

Rob introduced Emmanuel to Gerry.

'And we've got your wonderful father to help us if my wife does have any problems. He has been brilliant, Emmanuel. You must be incredibly proud of him.'

'Oh I am.'

Beatrice turned off the music and told everyone it was time for the birthday cake. The lights were dimmed and two of Faith's school friends brought in the cake from the kitchen and laid it down in the centre of the dining table. It was beautiful, with pink and white flowers piped round the sides and a big '16' in pink icing in the middle.

'Your mum makes cakes too?' Sandra whispered in Emmanuel's ear. He grinned and nodded.

They all sang 'Happy birthday to you' and cheered Faith, as she gathered all her cards and presents together to open later, after the party had finished. She felt it always seemed flat after a party, once everyone had gone home. If she saved her cards and gifts until then, it made the good times last longer. Not that their house was never completely silent or empty with them all there! She was thrilled to have her big brother staying with them for a few days. She noted he hadn't brought his girlfriend and was waiting for a chance to ask him about it in private, to see if something had happened between them. She was quietly hoping he had dumped her. Faith had never really got on with Natalie.

The following week was the School Sports Day. The school was divided into Houses and each pupil represented a House, so the Sports Day was to determine not only the individual winners of each race or event, but their points would also contribute to the team total to see which House came on top. The Houses were all named after famous people from Lincolnshire -Wesley (Yellow), Franklin (Blue), Tennyson (Green) and Newton (Red). The kids got quite competitive over their Houses, especially as the winning one often earned treats!

Louise and Jayne were in a few of the events, both track and field, but didn't expect to place in the top three. Grace, however, had been chosen for more and while there wasn't a Cross Country race in the Sports Day, she had elected to run the 800m and 1500m which were the longest races on the day.

The day began with the sprints, Louise managed a 4th place in the 100m final, while Jayne was 4th in the 200m. While these had been the distances Grace had competed in, when she lived in Birmingham, she had decided now to concentrate on the longer races. She was attracting some attention with her talent for running and the P.E. and Games teachers at the school were pushing her to join a local athletics club, saying she had a lot of potential to do well.

Unsurprisingly her races were watched eagerly by many, both pupils and staff and Grace didn't disappoint. She won both the 800m and 1500m finals for the girls with impressive times and in the 'fun event' where the top three boys in the school and the top three girls in the school competed against one another in a 1500m, she finished second behind her good friend and running partner Charlie Cook.

Afterwards people who she didn't know from all years of the school stopped to congratulate her or to say, 'Well done!' She felt like she had become a bit of a school celebrity all of a sudden, not something she was particularly fond of, but she had Charlie, Louise, Jayne and Toby to celebrate with and they were genuinely thrilled for her.

'You're getting quite the medal collection!' said Louise.

'Your mum will be thrilled!' added Toby.

July 25th was Jayne Stewart's twelfth birthday. She was one of the youngest in her year. For her main present, she had asked her parents if she could go to a Bucks Fizz concert and take Louise with her. She had been a big fan since they had won the Eurovision Song Contest the previous year with *Making Your Mind Up*. Both the Stewarts and the Thorpes watched Eurovision every year.

The big day arrived and the four of them went to the Festival Pavilion in Skegness to watch the concert. Jayne's mum, Tracy, had a rare night off from little Harry, who was being babysat by her best friend. This was as close to a date as Tracy and Ben (Jayne's dad) had got for a long time and she was planning to enjoy herself! She had even put some make-up on, though slightly less than her daughter seemed to be wearing!

It was a really good evening, even Ben was jigging around a bit to the music. Mike, Jay, Cheryl and Bobby sang all their hits including *The Land of Make Believe* and after the audience yelled for more, their encore was, of course, *Making Your Mind Up* – with snow coming down on to the stage!

'Thanks for taking me,' Louise said to them afterwards. 'That was ace!'

They all agreed they'd had a brilliant evening and it had rounded off Jayne's birthday perfectly.

Sandra was finally ready to go back to Book Club. It hadn't been her physical injuries that had prevented her going back sooner, she was doing very well in that respect. It was the psychological ones. She had first met Martin at Book Club, they had become friends there, she had even considered having a romance with him at one point, an affair! How stupid she was! But she valued going there, the friendship and being amongst others who loved reading and talking about books they read and authors they liked. She didn't want to give that up – and why should she? She couldn't let Martin ruin her life. He was in police custody somewhere, she had been reassured he would go to jail this time and she had many years to live yet, she was only in her thirties after all.

Ruth and Brenda had met her at the end of Whitlock Close and along with Mabel and Beatrice, they walked to the village hall together. Ruth and Brenda had missed a meeting too, as they had been busy settling Scamp into their household.

'Have you got that sorted out officially now?' asked Sandra.

'Yes, we've been in touch with the police and Martin has signed Scamp over to us. Everyone thinks it's the best thing.'

'And how is he getting on with the cats?' asked Mabel.

'Really good, thanks,' answered Brenda. 'It didn't take him long to learn the cats are in charge, so they're all living in a reasonable degree of harmony now.'

'Sounds like me and Nora!' laughed Mabel.

Belinda was pleased to see Sandra walk in and came over to give her a surprising hug. 'So pleased you're back!'

Sandra blushed and hugged her back. 'Thank you!'

Ruth and Brenda sat in a completely different part of the room to their usual spot. It was funny how people seemed to gravitate to a specific part of the sofa at home or a certain seat on the bus or the same area of chairs at a meeting. But her friends wanted to bring back as few memories of Martin for her as they could manage.

The meeting started with a discussion about the last book, then moved on to choosing the next one. Mabel had been asked to pick this time and she had chosen *Tess of the d'Urbervilles* by Thomas Hardy.

'Ooh that's a bit bleak, isn't it?' moaned Ruth.

'It's just a book I've always fancied reading,' explained Mabel, 'and never got round to. I thought this would make me read it. It was either that or *Lady Chatterley's Lover*!'

There was general laughing. 'Ooh Mabel, you minx!' teased Belinda, who was in great form that evening.

The same time as the book club was going on not far away, Emmanuel Achebe was knocking on the Smallacre's front door. Gerry opened it and invited him in.

'Hi Emmanuel, so nice to meet you at Faith's party. Would you like a drink?'

'No, I'm fine, thanks. Is your wife in?'

'Yes, she's in here.' They walked through into the lounge and Chloe appeared from the kitchen, drying her hands on a tea towel.

'Hello Emmanuel. How are you enjoying staying with your family?'

'Oh good, yes thanks. In fact that's what I wanted to talk to you about really.'

He sat on the sofa, Gerry did too and Chloe on the armchair opposite, near the fireplace.

'I've decided to move here. I mean, permanently. Birmingham's not been the best place for me recently.' He seemed to struggle to get his words out. 'Look, I'm so sorry about your son, really tragic. I sort of understand how you feel.' He looked up into Chloe's eyes and saw the sadness etched there. 'I mean, it's not the same, of course.' He took a big breath, letting it out slowly. 'My best friend died in the Falklands too. I haven't told my family, they didn't know him. I had a girlfriend called Natalie, but things weren't working out. I got closer to my friend – Ryan – and I wasn't sure quite what my feelings were.' He was fussing with the hem of his T-shirt and looking down. 'We were going to talk about it all when he got back from the Falklands. You know, what we felt about each other.' He paused and took a deep breath. 'But he didn't make it.'

'Oh God, Emmanuel,' said Gerry, touching the younger man's arm. 'I'm so sorry.'

'I haven't told Mum and Dad. They don't really know any gay men and I'm even not sure if I am. Ryan was the first man I have felt like that about. And I'm sorry to come over here and blurt this out, but I wanted to tell you how much I sympathise with what you are going through. I quit my job after Ryan died, I couldn't face things continuing as if they were normal, when normal was the last thing they bloody were!'

Chloe and Gerry were nodding. 'I'm going back to work next week,' said Gerry. 'I understand. It feels like everything should stop when you suffer a loss like that. It doesn't seem right that things go on. People eat, sleep, go to work… but inside, you're on pause.'

'Exactly. I knew you'd understand. So I wanted to come and tell you.'

'Thanks Emmanuel, that must have taken a lot of courage.' Chloe gave him a big smile, though fighting back her own tears and tears for this man's loss too.

Gerry stood up, as Emmanuel did. 'I work in property, you know, I'll see if there are any places coming up to rent in the village. You won't want to be living with all your family long term, will you?'

'Well, it is a bit of a squeeze. Yes, keep an eye out, thanks.'

'Have you got another job lined up?' asked Chloe.

'Yes, I'm hoping to be a teacher at the school. All being well, I'll start in September. I was doing my training in Birmingham and working in a primary school there, but it was a really dodgy area, I didn't enjoy it.'

'I think New Barnham Secondary School will be much better for you.'

'I hope so, Chloe! I hope so.'

They saw him out and he waved as he went into his family's house.

'Nice lad, that one,' Gerry commented.

Chloe agreed.

School had finished and it was the summer holidays. This year's Village Twinning trip to France had a few new faces going. They suspected it would have a completely different vibe to it than in previous years, when it had been a load of old blokes from the British Legion and the Smallacres.

This time, the average age of those going was much lower. A whole new influx of younger people had signed up - Sandra, Robert and Louise, Ruth and Brenda, plus Toby and his mum. His dad had to stay at home for work, as he owned the milk round.

This had caused a bit of a shuffle around with the village animals too! Lady Olga was staying with the Achebes, while Mabel was going to pop into number three to look after the cats. Ruth and Brenda had put theirs into a cattery, but Mabel had kindly offered to have Scamp, with the Achebes offering to walk him with Lady Olga! It was just as well their pet support network was so good!

As was usual with any of these kinds of trips, they had a four o'clock in the morning start. Louise had been grumbling about this for days and her dad had to agree she made a good point. Why did so many holidays have to start at such an unearthly hour? Couldn't they meet up at something civil like eight o'clock? Not that he planned to complain to the old guys running it, he had seen what they were like. They'd probably get him to do ten press ups for disobedience or impertinence!

Everyone had to meet at the village hall. The big coach was already there, and Dick Rayner was walking round, his smart suit on, moustache sleek, clipboard and pencil ticking things off lists. It was hard to see everyone else as there were only a few car headlights on to provide a bit of light.

Toby and his mum arrived and came across to stand with the Thorpes. Louise reached out for Toby's hand in the dark. They had already arranged to sit together on the coach.

The car park was filling up as more cars arrived, with some people coming on foot. There was an excited but quiet atmosphere. After all, it was a village, and no one wanted to wake up anyone who was lucky enough to still be asleep at this hour. Plus the small New Barnham police station was right next to the village hall and assuming the one policeman they had was still there, they didn't want to disturb him.

'Hi there!' Sandra jumped and turned round to see Chloe and Gerry there, pulling along suitcases on wheels.

'Chloe! You're coming too?'

'Yes, we weren't sure until the last minute, but I think it'll be a good thing to do. We always love going to France and when we rang up Dick, it turns out an elderly couple had to pull out for health reasons, so we took their places.'

'Oh I am pleased,' said Sandra. 'This is Toby's mum, I don't think you've met her before.' She indicated the quiet blonde woman stood slightly to one side.

'Pleased to meet you, I'm Wendy.'

'Chloe. This is my husband Gerry.'

She looked behind her. 'Oh, he's gone!' She laughed. 'That didn't take long!'

'He's with Rob, you might have known.' She turned to Wendy. 'Our husbands are best mates. They'll spend most of this trip chatting about cricket or something in a corner.'

'Trying to avoid us two!' teased Chloe.

Sandra smiled. This was a bit more like Chloe, rather than the pale shadow of herself she had become in grief.

'My husband runs the milk round, so he's had to stay at home.'

'Well, we'll look after you, won't we, Chloe?'

'We certainly will.'

Wendy smiled. They seemed a nice bunch.

Rob and Gerry were indeed chatting about cricket but had then moved onto pets.

'I see Lady Olga's holidaying at number nine.'

'She is indeed. Where are your chihuahuas?' Rob said chihuahuas, but the picture in his head was more like the three-headed dog of Hades, all snarl and spittle.

'Oh they've gone to the kennels. We daren't leave them with anyone. We'd come back and find we were being sued for loss of hands or something. We can't risk that. I mean, usually we'd have left them with Alfie, but…'

Rob nodded in the dark.

Dick suddenly clapped his hands, making everyone jump. It sounded like a shot in the dark car park and Rob expected the policeman to run out shouting 'Halt! Who goes there?'

'Right,' said Dick in an authoritative voice. 'I'll call out the names, you put your luggage in the bottom of the coach there, then get on the coach with only hand luggage please. Our driver is called Bob, he'll be with us the entire time, so please make him welcome. You can sit anywhere in the coach except for the front two rows. There's a television on the coach, though that won't be on overnight, and there is a toilet too. Thank you.'

As he began to call out the names, Louise whispered to Toby 'He's calling the register! Good God! This sounds far too much like a school trip to me!'

It was a long journey. By the time they got to Dover, there was still another eleven hours until they were due to reach their destination, a village in Sarthe, north-western France. They boarded the ferry and once it had set off, Louise and Toby walked round the deck, exploring and seeing what the other passengers were like.

They saw the Major with his granddaughter Pauline. She was at their school, a year or two above, and they couldn't stand her.

'Oh, I'd forgotten she was coming,' Louise whispered to Toby.

'She must have been at the back of the coach, I never saw her.'

'Me neither. Well, she won't want to talk to the likes of us anyway.'

Just that moment, the Major noticed them and walked over, smiling under his white moustache which he took great care to maintain in a well-groomed fashion.

'Hello, you two! We haven't met. I believe you are at the same school as Pauline here, my granddaughter?'

He put his hand out and they shook it in turn rather awkwardly, while introducing themselves.

'Yes, we're First Years – well, Second Years when we go back.'

'And do you think this trip will help your French?'

'Oh, I hope so, Major,' replied Louise. 'It's my favourite subject, so I'd like to do it for O-level eventually.'

'Splendid, splendid! Pauline here is doing French too for O-level. We expect her to get nothing less than top marks!' Pauline stood there, with apparently nothing to say. There was a pause, then the Major concluded, 'Well, I'm off to take the sea air. See you around!'

He walked off, Pauline trailing him a few feet behind, her long blonde plaits rocking with her steps, as the boat swayed from side to side. The sea was getting a bit rough and some of the passengers were starting to look a bit nauseous.

'Well, she's friendly!' said Toby to Louise, once they'd got out of earshot.

'Yes, she'll be a bundle of laughs. She reminds me of Sandy in *Grease*. Before the change obviously.'

He giggled at the comparison. 'Maybe she'll find her John Travolta in France and show us her sexy side.'

Someone vomited over the side of the ship.

'Yeah, that's my feelings too. Pauline and some hunky French lad.' She pretended to stick her fingers down her throat.

Sandra ran over to them, looking windswept and anxious. 'Have you seen your dad?'

They shook their heads. 'Why?'

'He went to the loo about ten minutes ago.'

Louise shrugged. 'And?'

'Well, he wasn't feeling too good.'

'I'm sure he's fine,' ventured Toby.

Just then, Rob appeared back on deck. Louise waved him over. 'You okay, Dad? Mum's been worried.'

'Yes, I found a good pinball game in one of the side rooms, it's a little arcade.'

Sandra hit him. 'Rob! I was worried. I thought you were chucking your guts up! But no, you're playing a silly video game!' She flounced off. 'I'm going to find a newsagents, get myself a magazine.'

Around two o'clock in the afternoon, they were on the coach again driving through Paris. Louise and Toby were staring out of the window at their first look at the French capital. There were lots of tennis courts, tunnels, sports stadiums, shops, modern skyscrapers and flats.

'The roads are hectic!' Toby was half out of his seat. 'Four lanes of traffic! Look!'

They were impressed by the Eiffel Tower standing tall and proud in the distance.

'Oh look, Sacre Coeur! It looks like St. Paul's Cathedral with the domes.'

Soon they were back in the countryside heading towards Chartres. Toby and Louise fell asleep, the excitement of travelling through Paris over, her leaning on his shoulder. They woke up two hours later when the coach stopped for everyone to get something to eat. It was a kind of service station. Sandra, Robert, Louise, Wendy and Toby sat together, the kids happily tucking into burgers, chips and salad. 'Well, if this is typical French food, we'll be okay!' observed Toby.

They finally arrived at their destination around six o'clock. They were exhausted by then. The village was a similar size to New Barnham. It had a collection of pretty houses around the centre with larger detached houses as they travelled into the outer areas. There were a few shops along two streets – Sandra spotted a hairdressers, a butchers, two bakers opposite each other and a small supermarket. There was an impressive church and a small school. She knew there wasn't a secondary school there, the older kids had to get a bus to Le Mans every day.

The Thorpes were staying with the Pellerin family – a couple and their daughter, who was twenty. They showed the English around their house - which was big! They owned quite a lot of land and two decades before, had built a whole new wing of the house on it, which essentially meant they had a sort of double house in one! They had six bedrooms, three bathrooms and – most impressive to the English family – a big games room with a pool table and table tennis table permanently set out. They had a quick meal on arrival, mainly consisting of bread and cheese, then went eagerly to bed. Louise couldn't tell if the bed was comfortable; she wasn't awake long enough to think about it.

The next morning, after a long sleep for their bodies to catch up, they had a long breakfast with the family. Alain was a bank manager, but not the stereotypically boring type. He was full of fun, seemingly always happy and a great host. He'd taken the week off work to spend time with the Thorpes. His wife Veronique was a housewife, less vivacious than her husband but no less friendly. Their daughter Nathalie was fluent in English, so she provided the words when her parents failed to find them. She was a language student and had just returned from a trip to Germany.

At midday, they all walked into the centre of the village for a formal celebration to welcome the English guests. This began with a church service in both languages led by the French vicar and the New Barnham one, Reverend Williams, who had come over with them for the Twinning trip. Louise found Toby and they sat together. She spent half the time looking round the church to see where everyone was and picking out familiar faces.

Afterwards they all went in a procession to the War Memorial, including the village band. Louise hated brass bands and wished she could put her hands over her ears but knew it would be rude. At the memorial, there was a minute's silence and a ceremonial laying of the wreaths from both villages, the Major placing the New Barnham one with great solemnity.

This was followed by processing to the Town Hall where there were speeches in both languages, playing of the National Anthems by the band and the signing of the 10th Jumelage (Twinning) certificates.

The formalities finally over, the brass band players left (as Louise silently cheered), and the buffet was served. While the Major and his granddaughter, Dick Rayner and the Committee officials continued to hobnob with their French equivalents, most of the other English took the opportunity to hang out together, sharing gossip between mushroom vol-au-vents with plenty of garlic, baguettes, cold meats and a variety of different cheeses, most of them smelly.

They were telling each other about the houses they were staying in and the families they were staying with. Ruth was explaining the unfortunate situation her and Brenda had found themselves in.

'We were shown our two separate bedrooms, both single beds, very nicely decorated. We explained we lived together, and Madame Debauve was nodding away, yes, yes, we know, but she obviously thought we were just friends.'

Brenda continued, lowering her voice. 'We didn't want to actually explain we share a bed!'

Ruth shook her head, laughing. 'So we thanked her and slept in separate bedrooms!'

Sandra whispered, 'Perhaps they don't have lesbians in France!'

They all chuckled at the thought, while one of the local waitresses brought round glasses of orange juice and champagne for the upcoming formal toasts. Leaning in towards the women, the waitress said, 'Oh they do!' and winked. This set all the women off and they were making such a noise that Gerry and Rob came over to see what they were missing.

The next day was a rest day, where they could stay with their host families or explore the village. Quite a few went into Le Mans to do some shopping.

The next two days were trips to various war graves and memorials, but Louise and Toby decided to stay with the Pellerin family. They knew this part of the trip was a big deal for the old soldiers, but it wasn't their thing. Besides it was dull and raining. Instead they spent their days playing each other, Nathalie and Alain at table tennis and pool.

On the Thursday evening, there was a big celebration disco for the village and its English visitors. There was a DJ playing pop music for the younger members there, plus a bar and a quieter room for the older ones. The former soldiers from both villages were predictably socializing together, drinking beer and exchanging War stories amicably. The Major was even wearing his medals!

Chloe and Gerry, Sandra and Rob, Ruth and Brenda plus Wendy and a couple of others from England all decided to stay in the bar, while Louise and Toby were already dancing in the disco. Pauline had abandoned her grandfather and was talking to a French lad about her age.

As the evening went on, Sandra could see Chloe was drinking much faster than she was and becoming more anxious and upset. 'I'll get the next drinks, Chloe. Would you like one of their Oranginas? They're really nice and refreshing.'

'Are they alcoholic?'

'No, but very tasty.'

'I'll stick to the wine, thanks.'

'Let me just see where Gerry is, I'll be back in a minute.'

The last time she'd looked, her husband was at the end of the bar with Gerry, but now she couldn't see them. She went out through the disco and found Louise dancing to a French pop song with Toby. 'Have you seen Gerry?' They shook their heads and shrugged their shoulders. The music was too loud for much of a conversation.

Sandra walked out of the front door and looked around. It was dark outside but the lights from the Town Hall provided something to see by. She edged round the side of the building where some young people were chatting, but they were all French.

Walking round the corner into the playing fields, she recognized Pauline's long plaits as she was snogging some French guy quite a bit taller than her. She was a tall girl for her age, but she was on tiptoes. Oh well, she was fifteen and hardly her responsibility, the Major had to sort that out.

She walked round the block without finding any other English people, then heard some noise coming from the smaller room off the side of the Town Hall. Following the sounds, she found the side door open. Inside was a Games Room similar to the one their hosts had in their house and there were Rob and Gerry playing a game of pool, pints of beer in their hands.

'Hey you two! I've been looking for you.'

'Alain showed us this room, thought it was the perfect escape!'

'Yes, well Gerry, your wife's a bit worse for wear. I think she needs to go home, I'm afraid. Getting upset too.'

'Ah, no problem, I'll come back with you then.'

They all headed back, walking through the disco and into the bar, only to find Chloe wasn't there, where Sandra had left her. They asked around, but it appeared no one had seen her leave. They gathered the other English adults in the bar together and explained the situation. Everyone was aware of the Smallacre's tragic loss and were worried about Chloe, and not just for the amount of alcohol she had consumed. They grabbed Louise and Toby from the disco, and all formed a search party.

Gerry walked back to the house they were staying in, but it was all dark and locked up, it was obvious no one was there. The others walked round the village in pairs, but it was night-time, and they didn't know the area well enough. They conceded defeat and went back to the Town Hall to ask for more help.

Gerry went into the midst of the old blokes and explained the problem to Dick and the Major. Dick got into organizational mode immediately, torches were found, their French counterparts informed, and they set off to look for her. The Major meanwhile was very annoyed to be disturbed from his long tales of bravery in front of his adoring audience.

'You really need to keep your wife under control, Gerry! It's not on, you know.'

As Gerry was stumbling for a decent retort, Sandra stepped forward. 'And you should keep control of your granddaughter, Major.'

'What on earth do you mean?' His cheeks were bright red with indignation, and he puffed his chest out like some bird squaring up to another.

'Well, when we last saw her five minutes ago, she was up against the side of the Town Hall, having her face snogged off by some tall French lad!'

Without further conversation, he gathered up his blazer and left the room in a rage. Gerry looked at Sandra. 'Well, he deserved it!' she said.

Back in New Barnham, the last few days of July were hot and sticky for Sarah who was four months' pregnant. Apart from that, she was doing well, resting as much as she could with it being the school holidays. Mark had to spend a week in London with his band, as they were doing some studio edits for their new album, but Sarah was managing well enough on her own. He rang her a few times every day telling her his news and checking she wasn't doing any heavy lifting.

She'd just been to post a letter when Beatrice saw her and waved her over. 'Hey girl! Come over for a coffee!' She crossed the road and went into Number Nine. Noah ran over to her and gave her a big hug.

'Well hello, little man, how are you?'

'Shall I put the kettle on, Sarah or would you like a cold drink?'

'Oh lemonade would be perfect, thank you, it's so hot!'

'Yes, you'll be feeling it in this heat.'

Lady Olga came running over and jumped up on the sofa besides Sarah. 'Hello, you,' she cooed, tickling the soft doggy tummy she was shown. 'How are you settling in?'

'Oh she loves it. All the kids want her on their beds at night. She's getting so spoilt!'

'She won't want to go home! Have you heard from Sandra? How are they getting on?'

'They rang the day after they arrived. The house is big where they're staying, the family are nice, so yes, everything seemed good there.'

'When are they back?'

'Couple of days. The trip's just a week. How's your Mark settling in?'

'Yes, he's all sorted. He's away in London this week for work.'

'And how's the baby bump doing?' She smiled as she looked at Sarah's growing stomach.

'Pretty good. I've got my midwife appointment tomorrow.'

'That's good. I always used to find them reassuring, knowing that everything's going to plan.'

Grace came down the stairs at speed. 'I can't find my tracksuit, Mum, is it in the wash? I'm meeting Charlie in half an hour and – oh hello Sarah, sorry, I didn't know you were here!'

'Hi Grace!' She finished the last of her lemonade and stood up to go. 'Right I'll leave you to it, catch you later.'

Beatrice got up to see her out, then turned her attention to her younger daughter's missing tracksuit.

Chloe had been missing for almost two hours and Gerry was becoming more worried by the minute. By now, there were thirty or forty people out looking for her, including the local police. Rob was trying to calm him down. 'She'll have just got lost. Gone for a walk somewhere. We'll find her. She won't have gone too far.'

'But you know how depressed she's been.' He didn't like using the D word, but it best described his wife's feelings since their son had died. 'She won't even talk to me about it anymore. She just clams up. It can't be healthy.'

'We can get her some help when we're back in England. Dr Chidi will know what to do. Let's just focus on finding her for now.'

Just then, a shout went out at the far end of the village. People were running towards the noise and Gerry and Rob headed swiftly in the same direction. They ran towards the river, as the French calls continued, too fast for the men to make out what was happening. An ambulance appeared, its flashing lights illuminating the scene.

Chloe was in the water, floating on her back. From this distance, Gerry couldn't tell if she was alive or dead. Rob held him back as the ambulance men waded into the river to retrieve her.

'Let them deal with it. They're the experts.'

They pulled her onto a stretcher and carried it up the riverbank to the ambulance. Rob and Gerry met the ambulance men there and asked how she was. Suddenly someone was there to translate, telling a tearful Gerry that his wife was breathing but suffering from hypothermia. He sat in the ambulance with her, and they drove away.

Rob thanked all those that had helped with the search and they dispersed. He walked back to the Town Hall and explained to everyone what had happened – as much as he knew. Then he walked back to the Pellerin's house with Louise and Sandra, holding them tight.

The midwife appointment had gone well, all of Sarah's checks were fine and the baby was growing as expected. But by mid-afternoon, Sarah wasn't feeling very well. She had been experiencing some dizziness and nausea, so she had a lie down on her bed and hoped she'd feel better after a rest. But when she woke up, she felt even worse. She was hit with sudden stomach cramps that bent her over and when she went to the toilet, she realised she was bleeding.

When she was able to move from the bathroom, she walked gingerly downstairs and rang her midwife who said she'd send an ambulance. She rang Mark too, but it just kept ringing. There was no answer.

Chloe was being kept in hospital for a few days but would be okay. Gerry was staying with her as much as he was able to, and their host family had kindly extended the invitation for him to stay with them as long as he needed to. The rest of the English were going home the next morning as planned.

The doctors at the hospital couldn't answer his questions. They didn't know if she had just been drunk and fallen into the river, or if it had been a suicide attempt. But he realised his wife was going to need professional help to deal with her grief. He couldn't help her by himself any longer. He had tried his best to do that until now, but it hadn't been enough. He hadn't been enough.

The rest of the English were very subdued as they got ready to leave the French village and their host families. Rather poignantly, there was a power cut that morning, so the French and English families ate their final breakfasts together by candlelight. After tearful goodbyes at the car park, the coach set off on its long journey back.

This journey felt somehow longer than the one there. This time, Louise and Toby weren't so excited about travelling through Paris and they slept more in the coach than they had on the way over. The ferry crossing was calmer, but no one was talkative or having fun, everyone was quieter. Some were sad to leave their host families, some saying how fast their time in France had gone. But everyone's mood was tinged by what had happened to Chloe Smallacre. Whether accidental or intentional, each person's mind at some point considered both scenarios and pondered how close they had all been to tragedy.

They finally arrived at the New Barnham village hall car park at one o'clock in the morning. Everyone was exhausted, even though they had all had some sleep in the coach this time. As Toby and Louise hugged and promised to ring each other the next morning, everyone quietly got their luggage from the coach and got into their cars to drive home. Sandra, Robert, Louise, Ruth and Brenda were all walking back, their houses only a few minutes from the village hall, but even they had little to say. They were all thinking of Chloe and poor old Gerry.

As the Thorpe family bid farewell to Ruth and Brenda and turned into Whitlock Close, a black shadow ran out of a bush and let out the longest meow! It was Mitty! Suddenly the three of them smiled. 'He's pleased we're back!', said Louise. They picked up their pace, excited about seeing Tabby too. The lights were all off at the Achebe house. They had arranged to collect Lady Olga sometime later that morning, but not at one o'clock, despite Louise saying she was desperate to see her dog again!

Tabina was waiting at the back door for them. They went inside and gave the cats lots of fuss before turning to the pile of letters on the doormat.

It was a similar scene at Ruth and Brenda's, but without the cats who were still at the Cattery, while Scamp was still at Mabel's. 'It seems so quiet in here!'

'I know. No meows or purrs or asking for Whiskas!'

Brenda sat on the sofa and took a few deep breaths. Her luggage was heavy, and she was aware at that moment that she was more than a few pounds overweight. Ruth had gone to put the kettle on for a restorative cup of tea. They were wide awake now and had to get sleepy again before they could go to bed.

'It'll be good to be able to share a bed again!'

Ruth laughed, picking up the mail from the doormat. 'It certainly will.'

She handed Brenda a couple of letters addressed to her, put the phone bill on the side table and examined a letter for her in handwriting she didn't recognize.

'Anything interesting?' asked Brenda.

'I'm not sure.' Ruth opened the envelope and read the contents. She gasped, said 'Oh my God!' and re-read it again before passing it to Brenda in silence.

'Oh Ruth,' said Brenda, holding her partner in a big bear hug. 'I'm so sorry about Ken.'

'Heart attack, it says, while they were in Spain. Oh, poor Bryony having to deal with that. He wasn't that old either.'

'No, he wasn't.'

Brenda read on to the end. 'Oh,' she said, as she finished the final paragraph.

'Yes,' Ruth replied. 'Bryony's going to have to move in with us.'

The Social Worker rang the next day to go through the procedure. Introducing herself as Tina Walker, she explained that Bryony had been staying with her best friend's parents since Ken had been taken into hospital, and subsequently died, but they didn't have the room to keep her indefinitely. Ruth was obviously Bryony's next of kin, so it seemed the best place for her to go.

Tina continued delicately. 'Now we understand there was an issue with Bryony not getting on with your current partner?'

'No, that's not right,' interrupted Ruth. 'She's never met my partner. She was told by her father that I shouldn't have left him because I was breaking our marital laws in the eyes of God. The fact I left him for a woman, not another man, just rubbed salt into his wounded ego.'

Tina sounded unable to process this relationship option and after an embarrassingly long pause, she just continued through her checklist on the form in front of her. 'How many bedrooms are there in the property?'

'Two, so we have a permanent spare room for friends or family who want to come over. Obviously that could be Bryony's bedroom.'

Tick.

'Any pets?'

'Yes, cats and a dog. Is that an issue?'

'No, Bryony doesn't have any allergies or phobias about pets. It's just on the form.'

More questions were asked and answered, more ticks were added.

'Is there a suitable school for Bryony?'

'Yes, New Barnham Secondary School. It's walking distance from our house and has a good reputation.'

'Excellent. We'd need to get her registered there to start in September. Now do you have any questions?'

The most important one, thought Ruth. 'When will she be moving in?'

There was a pause. Ruth suspected Tina was counting ticks. 'Well, everything seems in order, so probably next week. I'll talk to Bryony and her friend's parents and get back to you in a day or two.'

Brenda returned from collecting Scamp from Mabel's. She walked in while Ruth was still sitting by the telephone. 'Everything okay?' she asked.

Ruth nodded. 'We've got to get prepared for our teenager moving in.'

'When?'

'Next week!'

Life was going to change for them both and although Ruth couldn't wait to get to know her daughter again, she was also nervous and knew this was going to bring about huge changes to their lives. She vehemently hoped it wouldn't destroy the wonderful relationship she had with Brenda.

Sarah was woken up by Mark rushing in, stressed and sweaty. He came over to her, held her with care and gave her a gentle kiss. She half-heartedly kissed him back. She still felt tired and sore.

'I'm so sorry, Sarah, so sorry.' To his embarrassment, he couldn't stem the tears. He had planned to be so brave for her, but now he had seen her and her empty stomach, he couldn't contain his grief. 'I should have been there. You had to go through that nightmare alone.'

'It's okay. The nurses were great, they held my hand, saw me through it. I wasn't alone.'

'But I should have been here. I needed to be with you.'

She held him as tight as she could without it hurting. She hated seeing him cry like this. Her tears and come and gone and she was empty of them. She felt numb and raw. She squeezed him to her, stroking his back and muttering 'It'll be okay' as she would have done to her baby, if she'd been given the chance.

August 1982

The school holidays continued. Louise went to her Nanna's and Grandma's house every week, to give her mum a break, and she also met up with Jayne, Toby, Grace and Faith regularly. Grace was still running regularly with Charlie and was planning to go to his athletics club in September for a trial.

Gymnastics club was still going, though several of the girls were away over the summer, so classes were smaller than usual. Louise and Jayne were doing the extra squad training sessions now, ready for the new competition season which would start in September. They were consolidating the routines they had and working on a few new skills and combinations which they hoped would be consistent enough to try them out in competition come the autumn. The coaches were happy with their progress and both girls felt more confident now, especially as their bars routines had improved so much under the tutelage of the inspirational Lidia Chernova.

Bryony arrived in New Barnham on the Sunday, escorted by her social worker from Portsmouth, Tina Walker, who was passing her case on to her local counterpart, Theresa, who would be in contact in due course. There were a few forms to be signed - the inevitable paperwork that comes with everything – which were done by the adults while Bryony carried in her luggage. It took her just a couple of trips and she loaded everything at the bottom of the stairs until Brenda came through. Taking two of the bags off her, she cheerily headed up stairs. 'Come on Bryony, I'll show you where your room is.'

Without any greeting or thanks or indeed any words whatsoever, the teenager followed Brenda, looking at the décor with a critical sneer. As Brenda went past the upstairs rooms, she gave Bryony a quick tour. 'That's our room, the bathroom's there, this little door's the airing cupboard with all the towels and bedding – help yourself to what you need – and this room at the end is yours.'

It was a lovely room, Brenda thought. It had been their spare, so they had decorated it in a tasteful baby blue with a couple of arty prints framed in a complementary dark blue. Besides the bed, all remade with fresh bedding for her, there was a wardrobe, chest of drawers, dressing table with a mirror, a chair and even a portable television.

'Welcome to your room! All of this is yours. Put your stuff away wherever and however you like.'

Ruth clattered up the stairs carrying more of Bryony's luggage. 'Ah, you've found your room. Brilliant! What do you think, Bryony?'

Bryony shrugged.

'Your social worker's about to go. Have you got everything you need out of her car?'

A nod.

'Do you want to go and say goodbye to her?'

She shrugged but went downstairs, nonetheless.

'Well, she's chatty!' quipped Brenda to Ruth.

Ruth shrugged in reply and they both laughed. They had to keep their sense of humour. They weren't expecting an easy journey.

One evening, Hugh popped over to the Achebe's house and asked to talk to Chidi, who invited him in for coffee and a cake which Beatrice had made earlier that day. As usual, the house was noisy and busy, but they managed to find a reasonably quiet corner to have a chat.

'How are you doing, Hugh?'

'Yeah, I'm good, thanks. The medication and counselling are helping, I'm feeling much stronger.'

'I've seen you taking the dogs out every day.'

'Yes, dog walks in the fresh air. As you said, very therapeutic. Blow the cobwebs off and all that.'

There was a pause as Raymond ran through the house looking for a vitally important toy. The men sipped their coffee until the boy had gone back upstairs.

'So,' continued Hugh. 'I wanted your advice. Professionally, I suppose.'

Chidi nodded.

'Or should I make an appointment? Come to the surgery instead?'

Hugh started to stand up, suddenly unsure, but Chidi put his hand on the other man's arm and smiled. 'Of course not. You're a friend and a neighbour, not just a patient. You're always welcome here, you know that.'

Hugh put his cup on the table and steepled his fingers, avoiding the doctor's gaze.

'I've been offered another television role,' he said quietly.

'Well, that's great, Hugh!' Hugh looked directly at him. 'Isn't it?'

'That's just it, Chidi, I don't know. I mean, I could certainly do with the money, and it'd be good to work again.'

'What's the role?'

'Oh it's quite a good one, could be regular work, decent wage, nice part.'

'But you're not sure about your mental health? If you're ready for more exposure, more tabloid headlines?'

'Spot on. Exactly that.'

'How long's the contract for?'

'Four weeks initially with an option for a rolling six-month contract if it all goes well.'

Chidi collected both cups, put them on the side in the kitchen and returned, sitting down with a sigh.

'It sounds like you want to do it.'

'Oh I do. On many levels.'

'So why not try it for the month, then see how you feel? You can stay on the tablets, keep seeing the counsellor – or at least do telephone consultations, if you can't do them in person with your working hours. I'll be here to talk to, if you need someone. You don't want to turn it down, then regret it.'

'Yes, that's what I thought. Thank you.'

Noah came running downstairs and ran to his daddy, crying. 'Raymond's taken my train! He won't give it back!'

Hugh grinned. 'I'll leave you to it.'

Chidi stood up to see him out.

'I do appreciate your help.'

'Anytime. Really.'

He closed the door then took a slow walk upstairs to see what his boys had been up to.

Sandra went over the road to visit Mabel. She had only briefly seen her once since they got back from France, when she'd nipped over to thank her for looking after their cats and to give her a little thank you gift she'd bought in Le Mans.

Mabel was happy to have a catch up. She chatted about the fun she'd had when Scamp was staying with her, though diplomatically avoided the subject of why Scamp had moved into Ruth and Brenda's in the first place. She didn't want to upset Sandra.

'Are you still seeing Nora?' Sandra asked, sipping her tea.

'Oh yes, she comes over once or twice a week now. It seems quite funny how we didn't talk for so long and now we're really good friends!'

'I'm so pleased you've made up. You're neighbours, you have things in common, it's good to have a friend like that on your doorstep.'

'Oh it is! Talking of neighbours, did you hear about Sarah?'

'Going away with Mark, you mean?'

'No, before that.'

Sandra looked puzzled. 'Have they split up?'

'No. She lost the baby!'

Sandra gasped. 'Oh no, how awful! There's been so much sadness in this Close these past few months. A baby would have been such lovely news!'

'I don't think it's general knowledge. I saw Mark before they went away. He looked absolutely awful, so I shouted over to him. He came across and told me. They went on holiday the next day. I think he just wanted to take her away from everything.'

'Oh that's so sad.'

They sat in silence for a while, then Sandra asked about the book club and what she'd missed when she was away.

'Actually I've just finished the book, if you want to borrow it.' She got up and fetched one from her bookshelves, handing it over.

'*A Passage to India.* Any good? I've not read any Forster.'

'It's a beautiful book, yes, very atmospheric, worth reading.'

'Thanks Mabel, I'll get stuck into that then. I only read a light fluffy romance in France, so I fancy getting into something totally different. I'll bring it back when I've finished.'

'No problem, take as long as you like. We're discussing it next week at the meeting, if you want to try to finish it by then.'

'Great, I'll see how I get on with it. Right, I'd better go, Louise is due back home soon.'

Chloe and Gerry came back to New Barnham that week. Chloe had already started to receive professional help and was going to be cared for at home for a while, to see how they got on. She finally understood that grieving was serious, and people coped with the process in different ways. She had to give herself time to recover.

Chidi came over one evening to talk to Gerry and see how things were going. Chloe was already in bed so they could talk in private. The two men agreed that the treatment was the best thing for Chloe, and Chidi explained how good the specialist was that was responsible for her recovery.

Gerry was pleased to be able to talk to someone about it all. France had been such a mix of emotions for him, as he explained to the doctor.

'I was thrilled when Chloe said we should go on the trip. I thought finally she was on the mend, looking forward, able to find joy in something again. When we got there, she seemed fine, but then as the days went on, it was like she was slipping away from me…'

'Did she talk to you about how she was feeling?'

'No. Nothing. It was like she was only half there. There physically, in body, but her mind was somewhere else.'

'It's very common with grief, all of these things are, and every person feels it differently. Some people contain it deep within themselves and continue with normal life as best they can.' He looked at Gerry, waiting for him to meet his eyes. 'I suspect this is how you cope with it.' Gerry lowered his eyes again and shrugged. 'Others become angry, feel guilty, become depressed, numb, others become physically ill, maybe they don't eat or can't sleep. It's all normal, but sometimes people need a little more help, and this is why we need to help Chloe now. Professionally.'

'I just feel I have failed her somehow. I should be able to help her. I should be enough.'

'Sometimes it's just the right time for the experts to step in. It doesn't mean you aren't helping, or aren't good enough in some way, but those with a professional detachment and medical knowledge can offer something different to family and friends. They also have access to all sorts of facilities and help that you don't, as an individual.'

Gerry stood up and headed for the drinks cupboard. 'Whisky?' he offered, pouring himself one.

'Go on then, it'd be rude not to join you!' Chidi laughed.

'I was thinking,' he came back with two glasses of golden whisky. 'Has your Emmanuel got himself a place sorted yet?'

'No, he's still with us at the moment.'

'Well, I was wondering if he'd like to move in here?'

'Really?'

'I mean, he would be only next door to you, so close enough to be a big part of your family life, but here he can have his own bedroom and his privacy. I also think it'd be good for Chloe to have a young man around the house again, a bit of life.'

'Well, he's certainly quite lively!' he laughed. 'Though nowhere near as noisy as Raymond and Noah. Do you want to have those two instead?'

They laughed amicably and sipped their whisky.

'What do you think Chloe would say though?'

'I think she'll be fine about it, she'll see the advantages. I'm going to have to go back to work full-time soon and having an extra person round the house would be good too, to keep an eye on her and everything. What do you think?'

'I think Emmanuel would be thrilled. Close to us, but with his own space. Sounds perfect!'

'Great! Well I'll talk to Chloe then get back to you, we can chat to Emmanuel and sort out the rent and anything official then.'

Chidi finished his drink and stood up to go. 'Brilliant. Thanks so much and remember, Gerry, we're literally next door if you need us!'

Sandra hated gardening. Usually Rob did it, but he'd had some late finishes at work and there was a tree that really needed cutting back, as it was going over into Old Mr. White's garden. Not that he had complained, but she wanted it neatened up. Plus it was a warm August day, and Louise was out with Toby, so there was no reason not to.

She was up the stepladder and had cut a big part of a stray branch off already. She was just readying the secateurs for their next mission when she heard a shout and a crash from next door. Turning to the left on the ladder, she could see Old Mr. White on the floor of his living room.

'Are you alright?' she shouted.

She wasn't sure from this angle if he was conscious, but he didn't reply. She climbed up the next couple of rungs and scrambled over the fence, wishing Louise could have been here to vault over it. She ran through the open patio doors and to the elderly man, who was breathing but didn't seem to be responsive to her questions. She went inside the house, found the phone and rang 999. She explained the situation and gave his address to them, but when they asked her full name and date of birth, she realised she knew neither.

'I'm sorry, we just know him as Old Mr. White and I think he's about ninety.'

'Okay, an ambulance is on the way. Should be about five minutes.'

Sandra went back to see him. He was still taking shallow breaths with his eyes tightly closed. She stroked his arm and said all the right things until she heard the siren and went to unlock the front door to let them in.

Everything happened in a blur then. They whizzed him away in an ambulance and on autopilot, she locked up the patio door, went out his front door and locked that behind her, pocketing the key.

Later that evening, she rang the hospital for an update, explaining she was his neighbour and had found him and that as far as she knew, he had no family. The receptionist checked through her notes and finding his file, she read through them. 'Oh yes. Rupert White.'

'Rupert?' Sandra said, 'We didn't even know his first name, how funny. Nor his precise age.'

'He's ninety-two,' the receptionist continued. 'He's done well to live on his own for so long. Does he own the house?'

'Yes, he's lived there years. His wife died and he's been on his own since.'

'Well, he's broken his hip in the fall, he's going to need surgery and I don't think he'll be able to live on his own again. I think he'll be looking at selling up and going into a care home.'

'Oh that's a shame. Thank you for the update. Can we come and see him?'

'I'll give you a ring when he's had his surgery, Mrs. Thorpe. He's in some pain at the moment.'

'Of course. I'll wait to hear from you then.'

After that, things moved quickly. Without any family, it was up to the medical staff and Social Services to assess Old Mr. White's health and ability to live by himself. He realised it was a lost cause and he would have to give up his home. He knew he was lucky Sandra had been nearby to help him, but she wouldn't always be. He agreed to sell the house and move into a residential care home in Lincoln.

It was only a couple of weeks later that the FOR SALE board was removed and replaced by a SOLD sign. It was a desirable area to live and houses there had no trouble in selling. Whitlock Close was full of speculation about who would be moving in and what they would be like, the kids hoping it would be a family, Sandra and Robert Thorpe just hoping the new neighbours would be quiet and not cause any trouble.

Soon, another removals van was reversing into the cul-de-sac and emptying its contents into Number One. There were a few curtains twitching that day, watching as the removal men carried in boxes and furniture. But there was no sign of the new occupants. They must be arriving later.

Ruth took Scamp out for a walk and diverted into Whitlock Close to see Sandra and Beatrice. She wanted to ask if they could bring their daughters over to meet Bryony, so she knew some of the kids at New Barnham Secondary School before she started there in the Third Year when the new term began.

She saw Sandra first, who was on the phone to her mother, but they had a brief chat and she agreed to visit the next day.

Next up was Beatrice. As usual, the house was busy and noisy and full of people – the exact opposite to Ruth and Brenda's quiet retreat – though things were about to change, she suspected, especially as Bryony's record player, singles and albums were amongst her most valuable possessions!

'Hey, honey, come in!' Beatrice greeted her with her usual bubbly enthusiasm. 'How are things?'

Ruth filled her in on her former husband's death and their daughter moving in.

'Wow! That's a big change right there, how old's your Bryony?'

'Fourteen in September.'

'How is she doing so far?'

'Hardly says a word. Stays in her bedroom most of the time.'

'She'll be grieving for her daddy, love.'

'Yes, but there's more to it than that. She's never been happy about me being with Brenda. I don't think she – well, approves, I suppose!'

'Pah! You love who you love, honey, you know that.'

'I do, yes, but like most teenagers, Bryony thinks everything should revolve around her all the time. She thinks it's all a personal affront against her. Like I fell in love with a woman just to destroy her life!'

'But it was her decision to live with her dad?'

'Oh yes, we were always happy to have her, of course, but that's what she wanted to do.'

'Well, hopefully this will be the perfect opportunity to show her that you love her and want her with you – both of you. She'll come round. It's all new yet. Is she starting at New Barnham Secondary?'

'Yes, that's why I came round really. I was wondering if Faith and Grace could come round sometime. You know, friendly faces and all that.'

'Oh yes, I'm sure they will, but Faith's going to Sixth Form, so she has to get a bus to Little Dereham for the school there. Grace will be at New Barnham though and Louise, Toby, Jayne…'

'Yes, I just asked Sandra to bring Louise over.'

'Maybe Jayne and Toby could tag along too?'

'Yes, I'll have to check, Sandra was on the phone, so we couldn't talk much.'

'What day's good for sending the girls over?'

'Any day's fine with us. We haven't got any plans coming up.'

'Day after tomorrow okay?'

'Sure.'

'Great! I'll send the girls round together. If I come, I'll have to bring the boys too – well at least Noah, he's so clingy at the moment.'

'Brilliant. I'll see them soon then. Best get back. Don't want Brenda to think I've left her as sole parent and ran away to join the circus!'

The next day, a small shiny red car parked outside 1 Whitlock Close. Out of all the residents, only Mabel noticed, as she was dusting her front room windowsill. It was a man who got out. He spent a few minutes looking round the Close, eyeing up his new neighbourhood and she was tempted to go over and say hello, but something held her back. For now.

He was of average height, average build, grey hair, wearing glasses and about seventy years old. As she watched him, she realised he was also incredibly good looking. She hadn't considered having any male 'friends' since her husband died, but this man interested her. There was something about him. She wasn't sure what. She might talk to him and discover he had a really annoying accent or a silly high voice or something, but what she could see was very impressive. Ooh, she'd have to bake a cake and pop it over.

Norman Shearman walked into his new house and looked around. How lovely the house was, in its beautifully quiet cul-de-sac in a picturesque village. He was so pleased he had decided to move here after his retirement from the police force. He was looking forward to less stress and tension. He knew he wouldn't miss being woken up in the middle of the night for some big crime that needed his attention.

He hoped he would make friends here, maybe join some clubs if they had anything he fancied. He had a good-sized garden too, he always enjoyed being outside and looked forward to pottering around his new one and making it look nice. He liked nature and would be able to look out through the patio doors, watching the wildlife. He was sure they'd have squirrels and hedgehogs in a place like this. Yes, he'd made a good decision, he was sure of it. He was looking forward to making a new start.

A couple of days later, another resident in Whitlock Close was moving house, though this one must be up for the record of shortest distance to move ever! After discussions with his family and the Smallacres, Emmanuel Achebe was moving in with Chloe and Gerry. Everyone agreed it was an arrangement that suited them all. The Achebes were already quite crowded, and it was rarely a quiet atmosphere, so once Emmanuel started his teaching job, he'd never get the peace he needed to do all his marking. But his parents, brothers and sisters were thrilled he would be staying so close, and they could see him every day. They knew he'd at least turn up for tea; his mother's cooking was unbeatable!

Gerry and Chloe felt they'd made the right decision too. There was no way Emmanuel could replace Alfred of course, but it would be good having another young man around and that bedroom staying empty wasn't helping Chloe get over her deep grief. They all understood the benefit of someone moving in, making the room their own way, bringing their own style and their energy to the household. Chloe's counsellor agreed with them too, it was hopefully the perfect solution. Plus a bit of money was always helpful, especially as Gerry had been forced to take so much time off to look after his wife. It was still a low rent, so Emmanuel was thrilled with the amount, it meant he'd afford to socialize and save up some money too.

Sarah and Mark returned from their break away. They popped over to see the Thorpes the next day. Sandra opened the door to the couple and gave them both a big hug. 'I'm so sorry,' she said.

'It's okay,' said Sarah. 'We'll be fine. Thank you. The time away did us both a world of good.'

Mark added 'And we do have some good news to share.'

He held Sarah's left hand out to show off the sparkling ring on her finger.

'Oh my God! You're engaged?'

'Yes, we are!'

'Oh, how lovely!' She gave them another hug and held back happy tears. She was a real romantic.

'Any dates planned?'

The couple exchanged a look. 'Watch this space!' said Mark.

'Hopefully within the next six months,' teased Sarah.

Sandra offered them a drink, but they declined. 'We won't stay long, we just saw there was a new man next door to you, has something happened to Old Mr. White? Is he okay?'

'He's okay. Kind of. Are you sure you don't want a tea or coffee? It's a long story.'

'Well, if you're sure,' replied Mark, 'if you're not too busy.'

'No, it's fine, I'm all on my lonesome at the moment, so a cuppa and a chat sound a great idea.'

She put the kettle on and started to tell them all the news.

As planned, Faith and Grace went round to Brenda and Ruth's house – ostensibly to return that month's book club novel which the women had lent their mother. But the real reason was to see if two girls nearer Bryony's age could get through to her at all, see how she was getting on, if she wanted any tips about her new school or to ask anything about the village from a young person's perspective. After all, they were fairly new to the village themselves.

Brenda opened the door and after exchanging a few pleasantries, she suggested they go upstairs and knock on Bryony's door. Brenda whispered to them, 'She hasn't left the house since she got here, and barely comes out of her room.'

Faith nodded wisely. At sixteen, and as part of a big family, she felt she was fairly well-equipped for dealing with a stroppy teenager. Plus she liked a challenge! She took the lead and went upstairs, Grace trailing behind.

Faith knocked on Bryony's door.

'What?' was the curt reply.

'Hi, can we come in? We're Faith and Grace, we live nearby and wanted to say hi.'

'S'pose.' Was the grumpy reply.

Faith opened the door. Bryony was on her bed, reading some gothic horror kind of book by an author she didn't recognize. She was still in her pyjamas even though it was early afternoon. Her hair looked like it hadn't been brushed and the room had a slightly sweaty whiff to it, discernible under what smelled like half a can of cheap fruity perfume.

Faith waited, watching Bryony's face. Grace stayed slightly behind her big sister, peering round the side of her.

It was Bryony who eventually spoke. 'I know why you're here.'

Faith recognized the defensive tone. 'Oh yeah? Why's that then?'

'Mum and that woman sent you.'

'What woman?'

'My mother's … woman.'

'Oh Brenda?'

'Yes. Her.'

'Well, that doesn't sound very grateful of you. They've taken you in, after all. You should at least show them some respect.'

Bryony huffed, refusing to look at the girls. Faith wasn't fazed by the attitude, she had seen it before. She had nothing to lose, she personally felt the girl was just moody and selfish. She didn't need anything from Bryony, she just hoped she could somehow make things a bit easier for Ruth and Brenda, who she had a lot of time for.

Suddenly Grace edged round her and was looking in awe at Bryony's things – well, one thing in particular. 'You've got The Game of Life! Look, Faith! I wanted that for Christmas, but Mum said no, because we all argue when we're playing board games.'

'Well, she's right,' reasoned Faith. 'You and Raymond used to literally be fighting over Snakes and Ladders! It was a nightmare! Not to mention Twister!' They laughed over shared family memories.

The excitable little girl walking into her room surprised Bryony, and she couldn't stop a smile sliding out from under her couldn't-care-less façade. Faith noticed it and realised Grace might have made some kind of breakthrough here. Sometimes, cute beat sensible, she had to admit it. She'd never really done 'cute' – probably due to being the eldest daughter in a family of five.

Downstairs, Brenda and Ruth were straining to hear anything coming from Bryony's room. Brenda shrugged and Ruth whispered 'Nothing?'

'At least they're not arguing.'

They continued their conversation *sotto voce*, in case they could hear anything from above.

'She's hardly said more than ten words to me since she's been here.'

'Same for me and I'm her bloody mother!'

'I really don't know what to do. I was hoping Faith could get through to her, being a teenage girl but a bit older.'

'Yes and she's a good kid, sensible, got a good head on her.'

Suddenly there was a noise. Ruth clutched Brenda's hand, not quite sure what kind of noise it was. Then it came again, louder. It was laughter! They exchanged looks and grins spread across both their faces.

'I'm going to see if they want any food or drink,' said Ruth, getting up from the chair.

'You mean have a nosy?'

Ruth winked. 'That too.'

She ran up the stairs, pausing outside Bryony's door. Yep, definitely laughter. What a gorgeous sound it was, hearing her daughter laugh that way! She just wished it had been her that had caused it, but she was still happy. She had really feared it wouldn't work and her daughter would ask to go somewhere else, even if the alternative would be foster care. She knew this didn't mean everything was perfect, but any improvement was great news and she had to swallow down a lump in her throat.

She knocked lightly on the door and walked in. The three girls were sitting on the floor with The Game of Life board game in front of them. They were all smiles and giggles as they went around the board.

'Who's winning?' asked Ruth.

'Grace is!' replied Bryony. 'It's close though. I haven't given up yet!'

'Do you want any drinks or biscuits, girls?'

'Yes please,' replied Faith. 'I'd love a lemonade.'

Bryony and Grace agreed. 'I'll bring some biscuits up too.'

She went out the door. As she did, Bryony called out after her 'Thanks, Mum.'

This time there was no chance Ruth could hold the tears in, but at least she was out of sight of the girls when her emotions came tumbling out.

Louise was round at Nora's, having another sewing lesson. She found she really enjoyed it and the two of them were happily bonding over felt animals and looking through Nora's book collection to find the next project Louise could try. They were sitting side by side on the sofa, Tilly in-between them with her head on Nora's lap and her tail softly wagging against Louise's leg. Both of them would occasionally stroke her and she was content with that.

'Oh, have you seen our new neighbour?' asked Louise. 'He seems nice.'

'Oh yes, Norman.'

'Have you spoke to him yet?'

'Only over the road when I put the bin out. He's, erm, rather dishy actually.'

Louise howled with laughter, covering her mouth with her hand. 'Sorry! I didn't mean anything, it just sounds funny hearing you say that.'

Nora looked mock offended. 'I can find a man dishy, can't I? Even at my age?'

'Well, of course and he must be about your age after all.'

'Yes, I think he is.'

'Well he's certainly much younger than Old Mr. White, bless him.'

'Has your mum been to see him in the Care Home?'

'Yes, he seems to have settled in really well, thankfully and they can look after him there, much better than him being on his own in that house.'

Nora nodded. 'It was such a relief your mother found him after his fall. He could have been there for days otherwise.'

'Very true. At least Norman doesn't look like he's likely to fall over any day.'

'He's invited me over for a cup of tea, you know,' Nora said, shyly.

'Has he? Ooh, how exciting! Are you going?'

'Well, a girl doesn't want to seem too keen.' She nudged Louise, and they shared a conspiratorial smile. 'But yes, I'll make him wait a few days then I'll nip across.'

That evening, Sandra went over to see Mabel. She felt guilty not seeing her more often, knowing she was lonely sometimes, but the days just ran by. It was Monday morning, then she'd look up from her ironing pile and it would be Friday evening. She really wasn't sure where the hours went. *Tempus fugit*, most definitely. It was almost time for Louise to go back to school, for her second year there. The summer holidays had almost gone.

Mabel was always pleased to see her and the two of them talked happily the entire time she was there. They discussed the current book club title, the weather, Sarah and Mark's engagement, how Emmanuel was getting on living with the Smallacres, all sorts. They had so much to catch up on and the conversation flowed easily.

When Sandra mentioned Norman, Mabel's eyes lit up in a way Sandra had never seen before. How interesting!

'Oh he seems a lovely man,' Mabel was saying, suddenly all bashful and hair-twirling. 'So smartly groomed and well-spoken.'

'Mabel!' exclaimed Sandra, suddenly realising what this meant. 'A love interest! Well I never! You going to ask him out on a date, you dark horse?'

Mabel laughed in a high-pitched way that didn't sound like her usual self at all. 'Oh, do they do that sort of thing these days?'

'Well it's a while since I've been on the dating scene, but I shouldn't think things have changed too much.'

'He has asked me over for a cup of tea sometime.'

Sandra wolf whistled. 'Well there you go then, he must like you!'

'Or he's just being polite.'

'We haven't been invited over, so I'd say it's something a bit more than neighbourly politeness.'

Mabel was flushing red, her bright ears contrasting with her silver hair. 'Oh my!' she said, a bit breathlessly.

'Now I don't have to give you the Birds and Bees talk, I hope, Mabel?'

The elderly lady tapped her arm affectionately and could hardly answer for laughing. 'No. I think I'll be alright!'

'You'll be safe enough with a cuppa, but anything more, you be careful…'

'Oh, you are naughty, Sandra!'

That night, Louise was downstairs for a change, doing her homework in splits while watching television. Sandra was talking to Robert about seeing Mabel and how the elderly woman seemed to have a crush on Norman Shearman.

Louise suddenly put down her pen. 'Oh no!'

'What?'

'You said next door had invited Mabel over for a cup of tea?'

'Yes, what's wrong with that? Old people are allowed a social life, you know!'

'Oh, it's not that,' replied her daughter. 'It's just that Nora has been invited to his house too.'

'Oh shit!' exclaimed Sandra. 'And they have only recently made friends again.'

'Exactly!'

'Bloody old women,' teased Rob. 'They're as bad as kids falling out in the playground over which boys they fancy.'

'Oi!' Louise pretended to be affronted. 'I don't do that.'

'No, not you, but I'm sure plenty of others do.'

'And now the pensioners are getting in on the act!'

'Well,' said Rob, settling down with the *World's Fair*, two cats and the dog. 'I just hope Norman Shearman knows what he's letting himself in for.'

After the success of Faith and Grace's visit to meet Bryony, the three girls had arranged to meet Louise, Jayne and Toby up the village on the Friday night, before school started on the Tuesday. Bryony was keen to meet more of the kids from school, figuring that every friendly face was one less hostile face to deal with!

As usual, they met up at the village green, but there were a small gang of lads there they were unsure about, so they quickly moved onto the Chippie. They all bought cones of chips and sat on the Co-op wall to eat them. Bryony was quiet, but friendly enough when spoken to. She seemed to be weighing everyone up, getting an idea of them all before revealing much about herself.

They all seemed nice enough though. Louise and Toby were obviously together, she had noticed them occasionally holding hands when walking. All she heard from Jayne was her talking gymnastics with Louise. She gathered they both trained at a club and were working towards a competition. It wasn't Bryony's thing, she hated sport. She was more at ease when the conversation turned to television series and the girls started talking about how much they loved watching *Fame* and how sexy Danny Amatullo was! Bryony admitted she'd loved to go to a school where the kids started singing and dancing for apparently no reason.

'Yes,' laughed Faith. 'And even though it's impromptu and unrehearsed, they all know the words and dance movements perfectly!'

After they'd finished their drinks, they walked across the road, down a lane and took a shortcut into the park. Bryony hadn't been before but was impressed with the facilities. There was a big field where some people were walking their dogs. There were baby swings, three swings for older kids, a big slide, climbing frame and a couple of little sit-on animals for toddlers.

Louise noticed Bryony looking round. 'Haven't you been here yet?'

She shook her head.

'I thought your mum would have shown you round everywhere.'

'She hasn't.' Bryony didn't explain that this was purely her own fault. Her mother had been offering to show her round the village most days, but Bryony had ignored her or just refused to go anywhere outside the house.

Louise took over. 'Well this is obviously the park.' She waved a hand through the air from left to right. 'That gap over there had a bench thing on – I don't know what you call it. You could fit about eight people on it, and it rocked backwards and forwards. Then Susie from the Third Year decided to stand on it, instead of sitting down.'

Jayne continued the story. 'Yep. She fell off and broke her arm, so the council took it down and replaced it with a big fat nothing.'

Louise pointed out the clubhouse, which was shut that evening. 'There's a club and bar there. We don't go, but some families do, and I think there are sports clubs and things that use it – the cricket and football teams, that kind of thing. They play their matches on that field.'

Grace and Faith were on the swings. The others walked round the side of the clubhouse. 'And this is the beck,' said Louise.

'Oh it's beautiful!' said Bryony.

It was, especially as the light was fading. There was a stream which you could hear gently moving and a bridge arching over the top of it. Behind the beck were fields and at a distance, a few houses. Toby explained they came out further up the road nearer to the school. 'But we don't play up there because they get snotty about kids being near their posh houses!'

Louise and Jayne laughed, remembering when they'd tried to use it as a short cut one day and had been chased away by a rather annoyed old man.

They went back to find the girls on the swings. 'We've given her the tour!'

Toby checked his watch. 'We'd better go home, it's getting late.'

They agreed. They said goodbyes, Toby heading off back towards the Chip shop end of the village with Jayne, the other four passing past the village hall towards their homes this side of New Barnham. As they got to Whitlock Close, Faith asked Bryony if she wanted them to walk home with her, but she said no, she was fine, and it was only round the corner. They arranged what time to meet her on the first day back at school, so they could all walk together, then off she went.

'It reminds me of our first day,' said Faith to Louise and Grace. 'It was so much better going to a school knowing a few people.'

'Bryony seems okay,' said Louise.

'She was a hard nut to crack at first! It was all down to our Grace and The Game of Life, you know. Otherwise I think we'd still be at her bedroom door trying to get her to say something!'

Ruth heard the key in the front door and got up to meet Bryony. 'Hi, how did it go?'

'Good, thanks, they all seem friendly.' She fussed Scamp who had come to greet her too.

'Where did you go?'

'Just round the village. Chippy, park, the beck, then back home.'

Ruth had a warm feeling from her daughter using the word 'home'. She felt she was glowing inside.

'You'll be okay at the school. I think they seem to all enjoy it there. They're a good bunch.'

'Yes, I think so. Except for sport. Oh God, I hate sport!' Bryony rolled her eyes theatrically.

'What's your favourite subject?' She felt sad she didn't already know.

'Drama.'

That figures, thought Ruth. 'I think they've got some kind of Drama group there, though I don't think Louise, Grace and the kids we know go there. Maybe. You'll have to see.'

'Yeah, I'll definitely find out. Toby and Louise go to Chess Club, they were telling me, so I might try that.'

'I didn't know you played chess?'

'Yes, I used to with Dad.'

There was a silence. Luckily Brenda chose that moment to come out of the kitchen where she had just finished tidying up from tea. 'Anyone fancy a hot chocolate?'

Mabel had put her best dress on. She couldn't remember the last time she'd had the opportunity to wear it. It was a floral affair, mainly blue and just past her knee with short sleeves. Although she didn't expect a cup of tea to be anything like a formal garden party, she still felt she wanted to dress up a bit. And why not? Her hair looked good, and she'd dabbed a bit of pale eyeshadow on her lids, to give herself a bit of colour and hopefully a bit of confidence. She couldn't remember the last time she had visited a "man friend." She was quite excited.

As it got to two o'clock, she stepped out of her front door and walked up the drive. Checking for any traffic (though there was very little in the cul-de-sac, it was one of the benefits of living here), she crossed the road and rang the doorbell. Norman opened it almost straight away, he must have seen her coming across.

'How lovely to see you, Mabel! How charming you look!' He pointed to her dress. 'Blue is my favourite colour. It really suits you.'

She was doing the blushing thing again, she could feel the heat in her cheeks and ears. She hadn't felt so warm since the menopause.

'Come in, sit down!' He indicated a light blue three-seater sofa in the living room, facing a television. She looked round while he went to put the kettle on. It was neat and tidy, it certainly looked like he was on top of the housework. He had some bookshelves, a couple of arty prints and a big record player on the side table. Underneath it, there was a matching mahogany unit she could see was full of LPs. When he returned, she pointed to them. 'A music fan then?'

'Oh yes, Mabel, all sorts really. '50s music, '60s, classical, folk, easy listening. You?'

'Yes, me too. Cliff Richard's a big favourite, Barry Manilow, Engelbert Humperdinck, Barbra Streisand.'

'I like all of those! Excellent taste! Let me put something on in the background.'

He chose *Guilty* by Barbra Streisand, showing her the cover, before putting the record on the turntable 'Have you got this yet?'

She looked impressed. 'No, not yet, is it good?'

'Stunning! I'll play it, you can have a listen.'

'It's her latest, isn't it?'

'Couple of years old, I think.'

'I adore *Woman in Love*, I bought the single of that, beautiful song.'

'Yes, that's on here. One of her best!'

As the first track started playing, Norman went through to the kitchen, returning with a tray commemorating Princess Diana and Prince Charles's wedding. On it were two China cups with black tea in accompanied by a silver jug of milk and a matching silver bowl of sugar. Two teaspoons were on there too and a small plate of Custard Creams.

'Well, look at this!' she said admiringly. 'Tea, biscuits and Princess Diana! What more could a woman ask for?'

They smiled at each other. She was thinking how lovely this was, how promising he was…

Later, after they'd played the whole of the *Guilty* album, Mabel went home. After three cups of tea, she was desperate for a wee, but didn't like to ask to use the toilet in Norman's house, it seemed a bit crude somehow. She was just sitting down on her loo, feeling relief, when there was a hard knock on her door. Tutting, she finished doing what she needed to do, then got up and walked towards the door. The person was already knocking again. They obviously had issues with impatience.

As Mabel opened it, she saw Nora's face looking at her – an angry, accusing face with her nose wrinkled up and her eyes narrowed.

'Oh hello Nora, what's wrong? You don't look very happy.'

'That's an understatement!'

'Do you want to come in?' She stood back to let her through, but Nora remained rooted to the spot.

'No. I do not want to come in.'

'Oh okay.' Mabel was running through everything she could have possibly done or said to upset and annoy Nora this much. She couldn't think of anything.

'You're a hussy, that's what you are!'

Mabel took a step back. 'A what?'

'A hussy!' Louder this time.

'Have you lost your marbles, woman? I don't know what on earth you're on about.'

'You and Norman over the road.'

'What about him?'

'You were in there this morning for an hour and forty-two minutes!'

'So?' Mabel still couldn't work out what the big problem was.

'So? So?'

Mabel shrugged and began to close the door. 'I'm sorry, Nora, but I have no idea what I'm supposed to have done to get you so worked up, but I'm not being shouted at on my own doorstep.'

Nora put her toe in the way so the door wouldn't shut. She put her face up close to Manel's and hissed. 'He's mine! I saw him first!'

Mabel suddenly understood. 'Norman?'

'Yes! Norman!'

'Oh I didn't realise it was a competition.'

'He invited me round for tea.'

'Me too.'

'I'm going tomorrow.'

'Well I went today, and it was thoroughly lovely. Goodbye.' She kicked Nora's foot out of the door and shut it in one swift movement. She could hear her neighbour huffing and puffing outside, expecting her to knock again, ready for Round Two. But no, a minute or so later, she heard her walk off and slam her own front door.

Mabel sat down and laughed and laughed. What a day! She wondered if Norman realised the trouble he had caused.

It was the end of August. School would start in a few days. Louise was looking forward to going into the Second Year. It seemed strange to think she had completed a whole year at that school already. She recalled how she had felt on that first day, scared, small, not knowing anyone – and how far she had come. Her gymnastics was going really well, and she would soon become a teenager – at last! She had a lovely group of friends and the best boyfriend in the world. This year would be so much different, so much better. Bring it on!

Printed in Great Britain
by Amazon